Rogue Waves

presented to :-

Dave Taylor
winner
Men's Regatta
H.B.S.C
1989

Rogue Waves

Tales under Sail
from well-known personalities
set and trimmed by
Nicole Swengley
with illustrations by
Zeus

ADLARD COLES LIMITED
8 Grafton Street, London W1

Adlard Coles Ltd
William Collins Sons & Co. Ltd
8 Grafton Street, London W1X 3LA

First published in Great Britain by
Adlard Coles Ltd 1985

British Library Cataloguing in Publication Data
Swengley, Nicole
Rogue waves: tales under sail from well-known
personalities.
1. Sailing—Anecdotes, facetiae, satire, etc.
I. Title
797.1'24   GV811

ISBN 0-229-11751-1

Typeset by Columns of Reading
Printed and bound in Great Britain by
Billings and Sons Ltd, Worcester

Thanks are due to the following who have kindly waived payments:
Futura, Hodder & Stoughton, Hutchinson, Methuen, *Punch*, Sheldon Press,
Weidenfeld (Publishers) Ltd, The Sail Training Association and *Yachts and
Yachting*.

Contents

Preface

I would almost certainly have never sailed had I not gone to Plymouth at the start of The Observer Singlehanded Transatlantic Race in 1980 to work in the race press office. Here, in the carnival atmosphere at Millbay Dock, I met a colourful bunch of competitors, gazed at their boats – and the seeds of future happiness and excitement were irreversibly sown.

Returning to London was a dreary business in comparison. So much so, that I rang the Island Cruising Club in Devon and asked if they had a spare berth on a boat for a week. Never having sailed before, I found myself on that grand old lady, *Provident*, a 72 ft gaff-rigged ketch, formerly a Brixham trawler. I didn't learn too much about sailing on our way to France but I did fall in love with boats and being at sea.

Back on dry land, I spent two winters poring over Admiralty charts and tide tables at the Little Ship Club in London as part of the RYA Yachtmaster theory course. Now I'm trying to encourage the practical side to catch up!

I have had so much pleasure from sailing and from the people I've met in its pursuit that I'm sure I will always look back with gratitutde to those hectic days in Plymouth, in particular to Bertie Reed who helped me recognise the warmth and special qualities of sailing people – 'the same in every port'.

Sailing teaches one all kinds of things in many different ways; it's as much a mental challenge as a physical one, yet has a spiritual side too. It can also be incredibly funny and the stories in this collection go some way towards showing its varied aspects. They come from a spectrum of personalities one might not normally associate with sailing or with the sea; from actors and architects, comedians and company chairmen, authors and admirals, politicians as well as professional yachtsmen.

The refusals, too, had their own singular charm: Barry Humphries 'doesn't sail, has never sailed and hopes that he will never have to' while Brian Rix pleaded sea-sickness – 'I have never ventured further than the cross-Channel ferry and therefore have no anecdotes to throw up (sic) in your direction.' Stirling Moss regretted that his liner voyages contained 'no near misses, no man overboard and not an iceberg in sight' and Alan Ayckbourn admitted:

'Alas (or perhaps hooray) I have never sailed in my life. I have rammed several cabin cruisers with my own engine powered (rented) boat on the Broads and I have been towed off a Thames sandbank by a small boy in a rowing boat. But I am a sailor who adores the fresh smell of diesel fumes in his nostrils and the quiet roar of the outboard motor. What's more, I never give way to sail as I have yet to find out how to stop the thing.'

This book will help support the admirable work of the R.N.L.I. as it faces the continual financial demands of building and maintaining the finest possible lifeboats for its volunteer crews. And if *Rogue Waves* helps the R.N.L.I. to save lives at sea and provides a little pleasure on land, too, then it will have succeeded in its aim.

Nicole Swengley

'What do you mean – you're going home to mother?'

Frank Page

Journalist and Broadcaster

ANYBODY'S STORY

He was a fanatical International 14 sailor who relished the challenge of sailing his highly-strung and powerful dinghy on the tricky and tidal reaches of the Thames above Hammersmith Bridge. She was French, independently-minded and not naturally a competitive spirit in the sporting sense. But somehow she had been dragooned into crewing for him although all their friends feared it would put an extra strain on what was already a pretty volatile relationship.

Trouble was, whenever they went afloat he became the archetypal small boat helmsman, bellowing orders at the crew and turning the air blue when things went wrong. She suffered it in silence for a long time – she must have been devoted to him – until one day he plumbed the limits of her compliance.

It was a raw spring morning with the wind slicing across the water off Chiswick Eyot as if it had come straight from the Siberian Steppes. On the 14, things were not going well. They were last in the fleet, having muffed the start.

'You're standing on the sheet, woman,' he roared. 'Can't you get your weight out? I can't trim the bloody boat alone. Get the plate right down, for God's sake.'

She, hampered by the many layers she was wearing, struggled to do as he asked, her hands clumsy with cold.

'Ready about! For pity's sake, get a move on!' he screamed.

As they sailed off on the other tack, she turned and said, with measured menace, 'If you shout at me like that just once more, I shall step off the boat and you can sail it on your own.'

Of course he didn't believe her.

Seconds later, he was bellowing again:

'Good grief, get that sheet in tight, woman!'

No more words, she simply let the sheet go, swung her legs round and dropped over the side. He was suddenly leaping about the boat, struggling desperately to stave off a capsize, grabbing for the sheet, eyes wide in panic. She dog-paddled gamely towards the shore while he careered away in a maelstrom of flapping sails, dancing ropes and a torrent of oaths that would have made a Billingsgate porter blush.

Sadly for her dampened dignity, she went overboard near the Surrey shore and faced a long, cold and wet trudge along the tow-path and over Hammersmith Bridge to get back to the warm haven of the London Corinthian Sailing Club. But such proud gestures do not go unmarked: the rescue boat chugged across and brought her back, dripping, to the pontoon.

And he? Well, he had quite a time getting the boat back singlehanded in the rising wind. But he never bellowed quite so much, or anything like so often, ever again.

Their names? Oh come, you know that would spoil the story. Couldn't it have just been about any small boat sailing couple you know?

. . . — — . . .

Cliff Michelmore, C.B.E.

Television Broadcaster and Producer

BEMBRIDGE BEACH IN THE 1970s

Our daughter, aged about twelve, and a friend of the same age, both fresh back from a sailing course at Emsworth, are out in a hired dinghy putting into practice their new-found skills. They capsize and have very soon righted the boat. They capsize a second time. They are clearly in trouble and it is now obvious that the boat is sinking beneath them.

We prepare to go to the rescue when suddenly, to our relief, we see the 'nanny boat' from the local sailing club making in their direction. Yet in a trice it has veered away so we hurry to the aid of the two young girls.

What had happened?

The 'nanny boat' had approached the girls and from the stern issued a voice of pure cut-glass quality: 'Ah say, are you membahs?'

A water-logged voice splutters: 'Members of what?'

'Then you *can't* be membahs,' retorted the voice and, helm over, she left them to their fate.

They would, of course, have preferred to be rescued by the dashing Barry Dyer in the in-shore lifeboat but they had to put up with Dad and elder brother. Then they were soon back sailing something more stable.

Which club did the 'nanny boat' come from?

Well, if you have ever been to Bembridge you will know – even though you may not be 'membahs'.

Libby Purves

Broadcaster and Author

ROCK BOTTOM

No sooner had we hauled the poor little old boat out of the Portland Race (we had strayed into the fringes of it by skilfully misreading the tidal diamonds on the chart) than the overworked engine took its revenge and set fire to the floorboards.

No sooner had we doused the floorboards than a rock, awash, black and gleaming, appeared less than fifty feet ahead of us. The boat was all trussed up for a run, preventers everywhere and a degree of chaos in the fastening of them. We got them off in time to swerve and looked round to see the rock move, heave, and vanish again.

It was a submarine, diving just outside Portland Naval Base. And it was half an hour before we could bring ourselves to laugh.

· · · — — · ·

'It's a bit late for dive dive dive isn't it?'

H.R.H. The Duke of Edinburgh, K.G., K.T.

GOING ABOUT IN A WHALER

Just before the war it was possible to join the Navy either by going to the Royal Naval College at Dartmouth, age thirteen, or at about seventeen by what was known as 'Special Entry' after taking the Civil Service examination. Up until 1939, the Special Entry Cadets went straight to the training cruiser, H.M.S. *Frobisher*, where they joined the Cadets leaving Dartmouth. With the outbreak of war looking more and more likely, the training crusier was called back to be prepared for active service and so the Special Entry Cadets joining in the summer of 1939 found themselves occupying the Sandquay barrack blocks halfway down the hill from the College at Dartmouth.

We were kept pretty active during the course which concentrated on all things nautical. We slept in hammocks and were subjected to a great deal of instruction in seamanship, including boatwork, and we received the generous sum of one shilling a day.

The boats available were 32 ft service cutters and 25 ft service whalers and these we learned to pull (i.e. row with oars) and to sail. Each boat was normally in charge of one of our instructing officers but it so happened that I had sailed similar boats at school on the Moray Firth and, as one of only about three or four cadets in my entry who had any such experience and as there were not enough officers to go round, I was fortunate enough to be allowed to steer one of the boats while the others acted as crew.

About once a week, weather permitting, we all piled into the boats and sailed down the river to the open sea. Towards the end of term we were sufficiently competent to be able to race the whalers. The crew of a whaler was five plus a helmsman; a slightly curious arrangement when pulling the boat as there were three oars on one side and two on the other.

The boats were very nice to sail except for going about which needed good drill and a certain amount of skill. The problem was that whalers had a 'dipping lug' mainsail which meant that each time you went about the sail had to be partially lowered, the yard dipped around the mast and then hoisted again. This kept the crew pretty occupied. Meanwhile all the helmsman had to do was to put the helm down and hope for the best – that is, until you discovered that the process of going about could be considerably speeded up by pushing the mizzen boom to windward.

The technique that I developed for this manoeuvre, although not exactly very seamanlike, had the merit of working at least most of the time. The trick was to hold the tiller down against the gunnel with your knee while pushing the mizzen boom to windward. The obvious snag was that you had no hands left to hold on to anything except the mizzen sheet.

Needless to say, one fine day when we were leading the fleet the inevitable happened.

'Lee-oh!' I cried. The crew leapt into action and things flapped and crashed about while I went into my going about drill with the stern sheets.

I suppose we must have hit a wave at the critical moment but the next thing I remember was being towed along through the water holding on to the mizzen sheet. I hauled myself back into the boat and was sitting up to windward steering as if nothing had happened before the others had finished their operations with the mainsail.

When they eventually looked round they were puzzled and then hugely amazed by the fact that I was dripping wet!

I am glad to say that we went on to win the race.

· · · — — · · ·

Wolfgang Quix

German Competitor, Mini-transaat

AN ODD VISIT

I had been at the helm, steering by hand, all day. Ahead of me, the sun had set into the sea like a burning red ball. The temperature was becoming more bearable. The sky above was full of stars and alongside my small yacht I could hear dolphins playing in the sea.

This was the first Mini-transaat (also called 'Poor Man's Race') from Penzance to Antigua for yachts under 6.5 metres and I was sailing *Waarwolf*, a 5.7 metre Dutch Waarschip. To sail this small but brave yacht in the tradewinds was extremely tiring. She was more of a dinghy than an ocean-going yacht! She wanted to compete with the flying fish, go here, go there, but would hold no correct course. The Q.M. self-steering gear simply wasn't able to hold my *Waarwolf*.

So I had to steer by hand, hour after hour, day after day, mile after endless mile. Very often I was so tired that I went to sleep at the helm and woke to find the sails aback. But I was in a singlehanded race and there could be no rest. My boat had to go on westwards; every breeze had to be used to get closer to the finish line in English Harbour, Antigua.

The wind had increased now and *Waarwolf* was sailing westward carrying both main and spinnaker. I had strapped myself on with a lifebelt in order to stop me going overboard if I did fall asleep (remember, the yacht was very small!). The needle of the compass danced in front of my eyes and Morpheus wanted to take me into his arms – I could hardly avoid the temptation to sleep.

It was the first time I was crossing the Atlantic. I was deeply impressed by the absolutely unimaginable loneliness and the perception of how unimportant I was with my small boat in this endless sea. I began to look forward to reaching Antigua and wondered where all the other competitors were. I wondered whether the winner had already crossed the finish line and was celebrating his victory in the *Admiral's Inn* in English Harbour.

Occasionally the singlehander may think it unwise to trust his self-steering gear.

All the time, I was trying to stay awake, thinking of my family, of meeting friends back home, desperately trying to keep my eyes open and watch the spinnaker and the course. I couldn't even afford to leave the helm to make a cup of coffee or fetch a coca-cola because *Waarwolf* needed every attention possible. So I started singing, talking to myself, and singing again.

Suddenly, while I was singing, somebody knocked at my back, strongly and firmly. It wasn't my imagination. No dream this; instead brutal reality. I had my heart in my boots; my blood was pulsing through my veins. Goodness knows how somebody had managed to get on board this yacht, here in the middle of the Atlantic. Where did he come from?

Within split seconds, thousands of ideas ran through my brain until the thought struck me that I was alone and nobody could possibly be there. But someone *had* knocked at my back.

I wanted to jump up and turn round but I was fastened by the lifebelt which stopped me turning more than halfway and this only served to increase my horror. My brain told me that nobody was there and that I was having a nightmare. Yet, nevertheless, I had heard a noise behind me on deck. 'I'm going crazy!' was my last thought until I finally succeeded in getting up and turning round in spite of the lifebelt.

A big flying fish was tossing behind me. It had obviously hit my back when flying elegantly over the wave crests at night and was now helplessly struggling on deck. Still in panic, I grabbed it and threw it back into the sea. My fear gave way to enormous relief. I laughed out loud at the simple explanation.

Some time later I felt sorry for having thrown my breakfast overboard. What a delicious meal that would have been!

I stayed awake for the remaining part of the night without any problems. Early in the morning the wind decreased and the Q.M. self-steering managed to keep course. I could fall asleep at last. But before I got into my bunk, I searched every corner of my *Waarwolf* carefully. After all . . . you never know!

. . . ——— . . .

Kitty Hampton

Yachtswoman

EARLY ATTEMPT AT NAVIGATION

As children we used to spend our summer holidays in Polruan, a little village in Cornwall. We had a small 14 ft sailing dinghy which we spent a great deal of time sailing and, as it was one of the local class boats, we raced it a good deal as well.

One summer, we had a German boy to stay for the holidays. He was tall, blond and gorgeous looking. He was supposed to be improving his English but, being almost fluent, he did not spend any time studying. Instead, he spent most of his time in pursuit of my elder sister while I spent most of mine gnashing my teeth in fury!

Then, one day, I thought my luck had changed. He had been out with me in our dinghy several times already and was getting very keen – on sailing, that is. So when he suggested that we should go for a proper sail, somewhere other than just the harbour, and that Mevagissey, a small town just five miles up the coast, might be ideal, I was not going to admit that this was strictly forbidden by the parents and so I agreed to take him.

Off we set and all was perfect until we were almost there, when I realised that, of the two almost identical harbour entrances ahead, I could not for the life of me remember which was Mevagissey! I had a nasty suspicion that this could turn into an embarrassing situation! The truth was that the only time I had ever sailed there before was at the end of the regatta the year before when we raced there round a buoy and back again. As there was now no familiar-looking buoy to round, I was beginning to feel a bit lost – but the last thing I was going to do was to admit it.

I mentally tossed a coin, heads one, tails the other, and made for what I hoped was the right entrance. We climbed ashore, ate ice-creams and then, as we were walking back to the boat, he turned to me. Placing his hands on my shoulders and gazing deep into my eyes, he said, 'Kitty, why does it say "Gorran Haven" over the post office?'

'Are you quite sure this is the best way for me to learn how to steer?'

Christopher McAlpine, C.M.G.

Retired Diplomat

DOUBLE DUTCH

We were on our way back from Esbjerg to Gravesend in July 1939 in our chartered 22 ton gaff-rigged yawl, *Amulet*. This elderly, but noble, vessel had a petrol/paraffin engine which rarely worked.

After two or three days at sea we found ourselves becalmed off the Dutch coast within flag signalling distance of the Terschelling Light Vessel. We had run short of paraffin.

As we had a full set of International Code signal flags on board and a code book, we decided to run up a signal to the light vessel. Up went the flags signifying, we thought: 'Have you any paraffin?'

After a few minutes there were the Dutchmen's flags fluttering up their signal halyard. These, being interpreted, read: 'No. When is it due?'

This seemed a strangely Dutch reply to our simple message. So we consulted the code book again. We discovered, to our deep embarrassment, that we had misread the code and sent the wrong signal.

What we five brawny young men had sent, I blush to relate, was: 'Have you a midwife aboard?' We might have done better just to spell out 'paraffin' in Dutch.

'The flags say "Help, we're on fff, ffi". . . dammit, go get the code book.'

Michael J. Bird

Author and Television Scriptwriter

GREEK HOSPITALITY

I was in Greece looking for locations for a new television series of mine and, in between visits to various parts of the country, I found myself stuck in Athens for a few days with time on my hands. Earlier, over dinner at a taverna in the Plaka, a Greek friend had offered me a trip out on his Nicholson 26 any time I felt like going for a sail. That very hot Friday in June the offer was irresistible so I rang Nicos and asked if by any chance he was planning on taking the boat out any time over the next two days.

'No, I'm afraid not,' he said. 'My niece is getting married tomorrow so Katerina and I are flying up to Salonika in the morning and we won't be back until late on Sunday.' And then he suggested brightly, 'But you're welcome to use the boat if you want. In fact I'd be grateful if you would. I've been so busy we've only managed to get out in her a couple of times so far this year and she could do with a good run. Why not take a trip over to Aegina or Poros, perhaps?'

Well, I had sailed a Nicholson 26 before but I knew that there was no way I could handle one singlehanded. So, very regretfully, I was about to turn down his kind offer when I remembered that the night before I'd run into a couple of B.B.C. friends both of whom I knew were very keen and experienced sailors. 'I'll call you back,' I said.

When I got hold of Alan and Beth at their hotel they were enthusiastic. 'Great idea!' exclaimed Alan. 'Can't think of a better way to spend the weekend.'

So, early the next day, the three of us took a taxi down to the marina. I had been there once before with Nicos, and when I'd got back to him and said 'yes please' I'd assured him that I'd have no difficulty in recognising his boat. In the event, though, it took a bit of finding and it was only the name *Naomi* on the stern of an almost new Nicholson that finally rang all the right bells.

'I'll arrange for the boat to be opened up and given a bit of an airing before you arrive in the morning,' Nicos had said. 'And you need take nothing with you. You and your friends are my guests and you will find everything you need on board. Just enjoy yourselves.'

And he had been as good as his word. The sliding hatch in the coachroof was open and the keys were in the door to the saloon. Then when we got on board and looked around 'everything you'll need' turned out to be something of an understatement. Not only was there enough food in the galley cupboard to last for a week but Nicos had been equally, and typically, generous with the drinks he had provided. There were bottles of just about everything from raki and ouzo to whisky and brandy. Plus a dozen bottles of excellent wine!

'This looks like it's going to be a fun weekend,' Beth said, smiling happily.

And it was. The weather was perfect, the boat handled superbly and, each in their own way, both Aegina and Poros turned out to be delightful islands. We didn't eat any of the food on board – the local tavernas were much too tempting and far more convenient – but we got through a fair amount of the coffee Nicos had so thoughtfully provided. And there wasn't much left of the wine either when, late on the Sunday night, we got back to the marina and securely moored up the *Naomi* in her berth once more.

'What can we do to repay your friend Nicos for such a fantastic time?' asked Beth as we tidied up.

'The three of us will take him and Katerina out to dinner somewhere special,' I said. 'How about that?'

'Where do you suppose we ought to leave the keys?' enquired Alan after he had locked the saloon door.

'We'll give them to the night watchman on our way out,' I said.

But when we looked in there was no one in the little office by the gate so we left them on a desk where a cigarette was smouldering in an ashtray.

'He's probably doing his rounds or having a pee,' I said. 'He's bound to be back soon. And he'll know where they're from – the boat's name is on the tag.'

The next day Nicos called me before I had a chance to call him.

'Are you unwell?' he enquired solicitously.

'No, I'm fine,' I told him, somewhat taken aback.

'So why didn't you take the boat out then?' he asked. 'What happened? Or did you just change your minds?'

'But we did take it out!' I exclaimed. 'We had a great time. We took your advice and went over to Aegina and Poros.'

'Not on the *Niobe* you didn't,' Nicos insisted. 'I stopped off at the marina on my way into the office. Petros Yannatos tells me that he waited for you but that you never turned up. And the food and drink I had put on board, none of it has been touched.'

'*Niobe!*' I spluttered. 'Your boat's called *Niobe?*'

'Of course,' Nicos said patiently. 'Don't you remember? I told you, that day I first took you down there to see her, I christened her *Niobe* because that was my mother's name.'

'Oh, my God!' I said weakly as I did remember. 'Then who was or is *Naomi?*'

'What the hell are you talking about?' Nicos snapped, becoming irritated. And then he enquired anxiously, 'Are you drunk, Michaelis?'

I explained what had happened but I could tell Nicos didn't believe a word of it.

And since I wasn't about to lay myself open to a lot of possible embarrassment, I didn't make any enquiries at the marina. So there are many questions that remain unanswered to this day. Questions like who did *Naomi* belong to and why was she left fully provisioned and ready for sea, unlocked and with the keys on board? And why wasn't she reported stolen?

Well, be that as it may. One thing's for sure – there's someone, hopefully still about, to whom Alan, Beth and I owe a dinner. And at somewhere *very* special.

'*Chartered her specially for the Dieppe race, have you sir?*'

Sir Peter Wykeham

Chairman of Slingsby Aviation

A LAUGHING FELLOW-ROVER

When we were all young we used to sail from the Isle of Wight, and Dog Zulu always came too. He was a big blackish Alsatian, of a noble and kindly character, and though he might seem rather large for a forty-foot ketch we always took him with us. He was not all that keen on sailing, but he hated being left out of any kind of adventure. It would have broken his heart, and ours too.

Our ketch had an odd history. It had belonged to an old sea captain who lived on board. His ferocious appearance and his love of the bottle scandalised the locals, until one evening he came into harbour out of a rough sea, moored, spent some minutes on deck waving a cutlass and shouting horrible and defiant oaths (a frequent performance) and then went below, never to stir again. That is how we got the boat cheap. Its name was *Onward*, and we were naturally known as the 'Christian Soldiers'.

Zulu had two special places in the boat for himself: the top of the wheelhouse for entering or leaving harbour and when on guard, and a snug corner of the afterdeck for seagoing and night-sleeping. He would never come below; perhaps the ghost of the old captain bothered him.

It would not have bothered us, for not much did; not even the seaworthiness of the boat. We had no security worries, for when Zulu was left on guard it was so secure that cameras, binoculars, and hand-luggage could be left scattered around the deck. If any stranger so much as put a hand on the rail Zulu would silently lift his weather lip, allowing the sun to glisten from a row of teeth that would have done credit to the Great White Shark.

He became very nimble at getting in and out of dinghies, at climbing vertical ladders (with a little help from the man or girl behind) and at feeding off strange and irregular meals. At a time when post-war rationing dominated the catering our standby was to purchase a full portion of fish and chips – we ate the chips and Zulu had the fish.

I have been looking at a yellowed exercise book once dignified by the title of 'Ship's Log'. It was kept by one of us who suffered from uncertain spelling, and it seemed to concentrate unduly on Dog Zulu.

> *May 7*. Passing Needles. Fresh breeze. Boat rolling. Zulu wined all the way to B'mouth.
> *May 8*. Poole. Zulu barked at Harber Master. He asked us to move somewhere else.
> *May 10*. Kept awake by Zulu wining all night.
> *May 11*. Took Zulu ashore in dingy to chase rabbits. No luck. He is hopeless.

After a year or two, Dog Zulu became a very accomplished sailor. He stayed

'You don't suppose that nasty motor boat is thinking of coming alongside, do you Zulu? No, I didn't think so!'

in one place in rough weather. He tolerated cats on the next boat. With a helping hand he could manage even the vertical ladders at Newquay. He barked at Customs men. But all this time, without our knowing it, the influence of the old captain must have been at work.

One summer night we anchored in Swanage Bay, under a harvest moon, and drifted off to sleep after a hearty meal of Australian tinned stew. Only the rhythmic roll of a slumberous sea lulled us. One of the crew heard a splash in the night, but turned over and slept on. In the morning, misty, pearly, dew-soaked morning, there was no Zulu on board. Panic. The log-keeper's spelling went to pieces.

Sept 7. Zulu not on bord. Scanned shore through ~~bbnoo byooo bbnoo byooo~~ binoculers. No sign.

The shore was a good 400 yards away, but the splash had been remembered and gave the clue. Another more careful search through the glass, and a small black dot showed up under a half-upturned fishing boat. We took the dinghy ashore, and when woken Zulu looked only slightly embarrassed. Four hundred yards on a moonlight night was nothing to him, if it got the vibrations right.

That night seemed to change his pattern of behaviour. Thereafter he still loved to come with us, but he was grimly determined to sleep ashore. If in harbour it was simple, if anchored off-shore – no matter. It led to a type of entry in the log, still faintly decipherable, which became only too common:

Oct 4. Anchored Orwell. Rowed Zulu ashore in dingy. He wined all the way, but cannot let him swim as vet says salt water bad for his cote.

. . . — — . . .

Geoff Hales, M.B.E.

R.Y.A./D.O.T. Yachtmaster Instructor, Author and Broadcaster

FOOD FOR THOUGHT

The start of The 1976 Observer Singlehanded Transatlantic Race was favoured with light weather which was very kind to the spectator boats even if the quicker competitors were denied the chance to show their paces.

Just after the start, I was enjoying some cold lunchtime niblets in the cockpit while threading my way through the onlookers. I remember there was even a rowing eight well south of the breakwater, the weather was so calm.

I slowly passed a small two-man sailing dinghy and was surprised that the skipper suddenly shouted: 'It's alright for you – we forgot our sandwiches.'

I didn't really feel I was to blame and, thinking of the 3000 miles ahead of me, replied: 'But *you* can go home for tea.'

This brought the conversation to a rather abrupt end . . .

★   ★   ★

THE SINGLEHANDER'S REPLY

Approaching the end of the 1976 Transatlantic Race, after finding a way through the Nantucket Shoals and coming out of the fog to enjoy seeing land again, I sailed round the south-east corner of Nantucket Island, feeling pretty relaxed: nearly there, good visibility at least for the time being, and the boat not much damaged. I just wished I could call the Race Office to say I was coming and, if I dared, even find out what my place in the fleet might be.

Eventually a large charter fishing boat rumbled over towards me and obviously guessed I was a race competitor by the large numbers on the sails and hull.

Without any preamble at all, over the noise of his engines, the skipper shouted out: 'How long you been goin'?'

I decided that, in response to such a welcome, I did not have to give in easily, so I replied with: 'What day of the week is it?'

'Wednesday,' he said and then, to my amusement, sat there alongside while I sat in the cockpit apparently counting days on my fingers.

Eventually I answered his question and got the immediate response: 'Twenty-two days? Jeez!'

To which I replied: 'No, I said *thirty*-two'.

At which he looked horrified, opened up his engines and rushed away, before I could say more. So I never did manage to contact the Race Office . . .

★   ★   ★

17

ARRIVAL IN NEWPORT

I crossed the line about midnight and, feeling pretty much at peace, sailed slowly up the harbour towards Newport. Completely alone on the water, I could look at the smart restaurants on the headland, see the illuminated car parks and people moving around, smell the food and cigars (I thought) and sense the size of the bill. Maybe a nice idea for tomorrow.

Eventually I found my way to the arrival marina and was very depressed to see how many masts were there already. Although I always think I am last, because I know all the things I have done wrong, it is still pretty depressing to learn my worst fears are confirmed. There was not a soul in sight, though there were some lights in a nearby block. The only vacant berth seemed to be the fuelling point so I tied up there and stepped ashore. It was now about 2 a.m.

I decided I might as well head for the lights I had seen, and at the stairway leading to them found a sign saying 'O.S.H.T.A.R. Office' (I have since learned that this is not so much the work of a drunken signwriter but the preferred U.S. abbreviation for 'O.S.T.A.R.'). I went upstairs and into an office where a few people were sitting around looking bored.

One said: 'You just got in?' and I agreed.

'Coffee?' and I thanked him for the offer.

Someone put a kettle on. It all seemed a bit of an anticlimax after the struggle to get here.

Then one chap, less sleepy than the others, realized that my oilies bore a Union Jack and the label 'Henri-Lloyd Sportswear' – not a common U.S. insignia – and he suddenly said:

'Say, are you one of those silly singlehanders?' and again I agreed.

Well, Goddam, that's the first one got in unseen!' exploded another, and the whole place erupted into life and activity.

The kettle was turned off and a bottle found instead; my file was quickly dug out and friends – people I had never heard of – were phoned to be told I was in; questions and more questions. The initial anticlimax was more than made up for by watching the enthusiasm with which the organisation swung into action.

Eventually I managed to ask the vital question, though I was not looking forward to the reply: 'You're twenty-third.'

Twenty-third? Out of one hundred and twenty-six? In a small cruising boat?

'Where are all the bigger boats?'

'Well, we don't know. You'll have to sit here like us and wait and see . . .'

. . . — — — . . .

Major Pat Reid, M.B.E., M.C.

Author of The Colditz Story

THE PIGEON

The following anecdote comes from his book The Great Leveller, *to be published in 1986. This relates the story of the Sail Training Association, its many personalities including the first Master, Glyn Griffiths, and life on board the schooners* Sir Winston Churchill *and* Malcolm Miller.

★   ★   ★

The days were beginning to slip by quickly. The end of the voyage, I was told, would be upon us like an express train. Such was the influence of timelessness created by the open sea and sky: so big, so vast that it swallowed up night and day in sun-size mouthfuls as dawn and dusk pursued each other, leaving no landmarks behind. The hours of the day were more important than the day itself. One had to think twice about what day of the week it was and the date had lost significance.

Sunday came round on the high seas and was recognisable because Glyn held a voluntary church parade on the fore-deck. The wind was light but steady, about Force 2 and coming from abaft the beam, so the ship eased along on a fairly even keel.

Church parade was at 1100 hours and a sizeable gathering it turned out to be; about thirty strong, all in sailing gear, but little scruffiness was discernible. Number One had asked Glyn's permission to attend barefoot as he had stubbed his toe and it was very tender. As Glyn put it: 'I don't mind and I'm sure the Almighty won't either.' Prayers started with Number One standing one pace behind the Captain and with the congregation in a semi-circle in front of them. As Glyn began reading, a homing pigeon, needing a rest, landed on the rail and hopped down to the deck. Nobody took much notice of it. It stood still, bowing its head up and down silently, beady eyes observing everything.

Glyn intoned in his mellow voice his own adaptation of the Naval Prayer:

'O Eternal Lord God Who alone spreadest out the Heavens and rulest the raging of the sea; Who hath encompassed the waters with bounds until day and night come to an end: Be pleased to receive into Thy Almighty and most gracious protection the persons of us Thy servants. Preserve us from the dangers of the sea, that we may in peace and quietness serve Thee our God; and that we may return in safety to enjoy the blessings of the land, with the fruits of our labours; with a thankful remembrance of Thy mercies to praise and glorify Thy holy Name through Jesus Christ our Lord. *Amen.*'

By the time Glyn had finished this sonorous and moving prayer, the pigeon had become bolder and was the leading member of the silent congregation; Glyn continued with the Collect of Grace from Morning Prayer. The phrase

'He says could you please give him a bearing on Mecca, sir.'

'Neither run into any kind of danger . . .' rings sound and full of meaning on a sailing ship's deck as opposed to the quiet, safe atmosphere of a parish church. It was during this prayer that the pigeon spied Number One's bare feet and made a flanking approach towards the toes which he then began to peck. Glyn noticed some loss of attention to the matter in hand but could not see what the trainees could all see; namely, Number One surreptitiously marking time as each peck of the pigeon's beak struck home, with an accompanying pained expression on Number One's face.

Glyn launched into the Lord's Prayer, prefixed with 'Let us now say together the Lord's Prayer – remembering our families, those near and dear to us especially those who are sick . . .' The boys really joined in heartily. At the same time grins started to appear, uncontrollably as it seemed, on all the faces in the semicircle around him. He told us afterwards that at this point he was sure his flybuttons were undone and his trousers peeling apart, but he dared not look down.

He continued the service, with his own Prayer for Peace:

'Almighty God, from whom all thoughts of truth and peace proceed, kindle, we pray thee, in the hearts of all men the true love of peace, and guide with Thy pure and peaceable wisdom all those who take counsel for the nations of the earth, that in tranquillity Thy Kingdom may go forward 'til the earth is filled with the knowledge of Thy love, through Jesus Christ our Lord. *Amen.*'

His voice had an ethereal clarity. There is no echo on the open sea.

The pigeon had obviously had a long and exhausting flight and must have been literally starving because he was not put off by Number One's fidgeting at all and went for his toes as each foot came down. Number One was now *in extremis*, wincing with pain and almost running on the spot.

Glyn was concluding the service with A Prayer of St Chrysostom:

'Almighty God, who has given us grace at this time with one accord to make our common supplications unto thee; and dost promise that when two or three are gathered together in thy Name Thou wilt grant their requests: Fulfil now, O Lord, the desires and petitions of thy servants, as may be most expedient for them; granting us in this world knowledge of thy truth, and in the world to come life everlasting. *Amen.*'

During this prayer the boys could no longer contain themselves. Uncontrollable guffaws of laughter broke out. Glyn followed the direction of their concentrated gaze and at last realised the cause of the disturbance.

One look at Number One's pained expression as he danced to the tune of the outrageous bird was enough. Glyn closed the prayer book and rocked with laughter . . .

· · · — — · · ·

Peter Jay

Author and Broadcaster

CONFIDENCE TRICK

Cruising off the west coast of Corsica in 1982 I sighted an exceptionally large whale at a range of about fifty yards. It was showing at least thirty feet of back out of the water and must have been substantially more than twice that length altogether.

I called below for members of my crew to come and see the monster. My fourteen year old daughter, Alice, rushed on deck, gaped with amazement and screamed, 'Daddy, Daddy, get it to go away!'

I thought that this showed touching, if slightly absurd, faith in paternal omnipotence.

. . . — — — . . .

Vice Admiral Sir John Woodward, K.C.B.
IN A BIT OF A FIX

Amongst my less comfortable memories is one particular trip back from Alderney to Yarmouth.

I had intended to make passage overnight to arrive midday-ish off the Needles to catch the tide up to Yarmouth. A forecast of patchy fog caused me to prepare a contingency plan by which, instead of going straight for the Needles, I would aim for the middle of Poole/Christchurch Bay on a northerly course and, when St Catherine's Point radio beacon was bearing east, I would alter course to run down the bearing of Poole Harbour radio beacon, situated on the dolphin structure at the left-hand side of the seaward end of the long Poole Harbour entrance channel. I believed it should not be too difficult to find the dolphin and then either anchor or 'buoy hop' into harbour.

In the event, I ran into fog only five miles north of Alderney and should have turned back instantly. But I thought that perhaps it was only a patch as forecast – and started regretting that thought half an hour afterwards when it was too late. Motoring on, heading for the middle of the bay, through the cold, clammy fog was something less than cheerful work. Happily, the fog lifted before I needed to turn down the bearing of Poole Harbour beacon and I was able to revert to my first plan.

This was just as well, as I discovered three days later while browsing through *Droggies Small Ship Chart Corrections* for that quarter which I had left at home during my trip. Poole radio beacon had been moved from the dolphin to a building at 'Sandbanks', the appropriately-named large piece of dry land at the right hand side of the actual harbour entrance. So just where I would have ended up if the fog had persisted is anybody's guess . . .

. . . — — . . .

'I am sure we shall be there any minute, darling. We're bang on course.'

Sir Maurice Laing

President of the Royal Yachting Association

AN UNREPEATABLE EXPERIENCE

Last season, on our return from a cross-Channel race and after the crew had been well wined and dined, I had an experience the like of which I do not wish to be repeated.

As the saving of weight is an absolute priority in the modern racing yacht, *Bathsheba*'s loo is one of those lightweight 'pumped-up' contraptions instead of the good old-fashioned 'Baby Blake' and is situated behind the bulkhead in the open forepeak. It is the only item in the forepeak which is painted a brilliant white.

Well into the following morning 'nature' called but, being a cautious type and also fully aware of how well the crew had dined, I checked to see that the contraption appeared to be all clear and clean. To do this, I had to pump water in and out and, in so doing, the pump handle became detached from the plunger and came out of its socket. Inevitably, I was bending down to carry out this task and the contents of the 'last performance' shot out into my face as well as all over the beautifully white painted forepeak.

I acted very quickly and got the pump handle back into place before the operation was completed and screwed it down. Fortunately, I was wearing glasses at the time!

Somewhat shaken, I took off all my clothes, opened the hatch and threw overboard the most offending of them.

Within a few seconds all but the helmsman appeared in the opening, and were both horrified and hilarious in what they said. I heard one mutter something about '. . . covered all over in sweet violets'.

As there is – fortunately – a step down in the forepeak, none of the offending material got into the main cabin and one of the crew, having already given me some fresh water to drink, got me to stand under the forehatch and gave me a very good shower. I then used the rest of my clothes to clean up the foredeck to the best of my ability.

This crew member then helped to get rid of the remaining mess and, in so doing, also pumped up the loo and the same performance was repeated right in his face! When he, poor fellow, had dealt with his problems in a somewhat similar way, the heads were put out of bounds for the rest of the journey.

On reaching Cowes, there was some hilarity in the boat yard and the foreman was given the job of fixing the loo. Imagine his consternation and surprise when he found that the contents had not entirely dispersed and the same treatment – although not quite as forcibly – was meted out to him!

There are several obvious lessons to be learned from this:
(1) Do not allow your crew to have such a good time ashore.
(2) Stick to the old-fashioned 'Baby Blake' – even if it is heavier.
(3) Why go racing at all at my age?

Many years ago, the Duke of Edinburgh described ocean racing as being akin to standing under a freezing cold shower and tearing up five pound notes. I now have a new version!

. . . —— —— . . .

'Well, if you can't read French either, I guess we'll just have to take pot luck.'

Victor H. Watson

Chairman, John Waddington plc

DAVID'S FIRST FISH

Bill and Guy and I were certainly three men in a boat but, unlike Jerome's celebrated trio, we had no dog. Instead we had David, Bill's twelve year old ray of sunshine – although, for me, that description lost its lustre when David, at the helm, abruptly changed tack in a lumpy sea at the *moment critique* of my matutinals. I suddenly and painfully learned why the loo is called a 'head' on a boat. My head burst the door open and I was pitched into the life-jacket locker. How David laughed! But my turn came later.

From the moment we sailed out of Crinan towards Dorus Mor on that fresh morning in early September 1975, David had his fishing line over the stern with a spinner on the end and, even before we had had our first pink gin, he had caught a fish. Great excitement! David's first fish! He put it in a plastic bag meaning to eat it later. And from then on his enthusiasm for fishing eclipsed all else. In fact, he was a blessed nuisance! Always in the way, never hauling in quickly enough when we were about to drop anchor, but sadly never catching another fish.

The first fish hung about. David did not like the idea of gutting it and we all thought it too small to bother with. After three days, however, it began to hum even more than the sailors so Bill threw it overboard, plastic bag and all. David was most upset but he redoubled his vigilance at the fishing line, determined to strike again before the voyage was over.

Later that day we returned to Crinan after a marvellous weekend in one of sailing's finest playgrounds.

'Pull in the line,' said Bill, 'we're coming up to the mooring.'

The result was the funniest thing I'd ever seen. David had caught a fish. But not a second fish. He'd caught the first fish again – still in its plastic bag!

· · · — — — · · ·

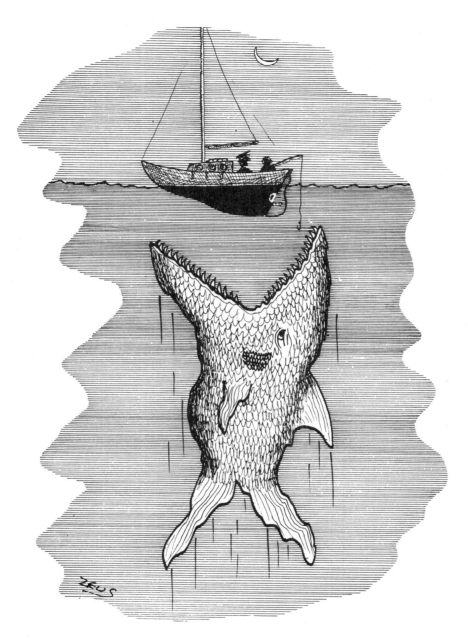

'*Let's face it, son, we're just not going to catch anything tonight.*'

Captain The Lord Mottistone,

C.B.E., D.L., R.N. retd

NAUTICAL NUANCES

At the age of about eleven (perfectly able to swim), I fell overboard from the bow of a small yacht anchored to the east of Hurst Castle. A grown-up cousin in the cockpit saw this and, with a cry of 'Man Overboard!' dived in and swam heavily towards me. In the meantime, treading water before turning to swim back to the yacht myself, I touched the bottom. By the time my cousin reached me, I was standing on the sand with the water only up to my chest. To my chagrin, for ever afterwards, the cousin has 'dined out' on the claim that he saved my life!

* * *

We anchored in early afternoon at L'Aberwrach after a tiresome passage through the Chenal du Four, intending to get our heads down for a couple of hours before the customary evening run ashore. Amongst the crew was a young man, hitherto unknown to the rest of us, who had gallantly responded to a Yacht Club request for a crew member. In the twenty-four hours that we had known him, our new young colleague seemed determined to show us that he knew all about sailing boats of all sizes and certainly more than the rest of us put together. He was scornful of our wish for an afternoon 'zizz' and asked if he could take the rubber dinghy with outboard and go exploring.

Somewhat unwisely, I took his 'great knowledge' about boats for granted, perhaps encouraged by the thought that a potential disturbance to our slumbers would be removed for a time. We assisted him in securing the outboard on the dinghy, tightly enough I thought, with the understanding that this was a *competent* seaman. Our colleague started the engine alright and off he went.

Within seconds, at full throttle, he put the tiller hard down. The engine flew off to starboard. The boat capsized to port. The driver was in between. A wonderful sight to behold! We easily recovered boat, oars and its crew. The engine sadly sank into the mud and repeated dives failed to locate it. It was only then that our super-efficient colleague confessed that, although he knew *all* about *all* other sorts of boat, he hadn't actually *driven* an outboard dinghy before!

* * *

We were returning from the Dinard race one summer in the Signal School yacht, *Mermaid II*, a Belmore. At midday on Sunday, we were becalmed in mid-channel. The engine was a small one with fuel only for entering and leaving harbour, so no way could we motor more than half the distance to the Needles.

In those days few, if any, racing yachts had ship-shore radio. And on the Monday morning I was due to give a lecture to the Naval Staff Course. How was I to tell them that I couldn't make it?

At that moment, over the horizon, came an aircraft carrier doing flying practice at high speed in 'no wind' conditions. We may not have had a radio but, being the Signal School yacht, we did have an Aldis lamp and several competent people to use it.

We called up the carrier and gradually, as she zoomed back and forth from horizon to horizon, flashed her a message to pass on to the Royal Naval College, Greenwich. I believe the signal staff of the carrier must have recognised the yacht and persuaded their captain not to get *too* far away!

The Director of the Staff College, who was a good friend, got the message in time to make other arrangements, but I do not believe he ever really forgave me for being so irresponsible as to indulge in the uncertainties of ocean racing when committed to that most important of all engagements – a Staff College lecture!

· · · — — — · · ·

Peter Phillips

British Competitor, La Trinité International Multihull Series 1984

FRENCH FARCE

It is the start of La Trinité, the big International Multihull race. The fancied British entry, *Travacrest Seaway*, glides serenely towards the start-line weaving deftly through the busy congestion of thirty competing multihulls. It is blowing quite hard as the start-line approaches and, responding to a sudden wind change, the yacht moves on to a port bias. Then, gathering speed, *Travacrest Seaway* flips to the windward end of the line, steering well away from the committee boat.

With 24 knots of wind gusting, the whole line of yachts unexpectedly luffs up, including *Travacrest Seaway* which flounces sweetly not only past the limit line but also straight into and over the motor boat perched at the end of the line keeping a look-out for infringements.

Pernods disperse at one fell swoop, the wheelhouse lifts off completely, and three committee members plunge overboard and into the sea – a drama performed to the unsavoury strains of a symphony of harsh grinding noises.

Out at sea, the race is now three miles away. Closer inshore, surviving committee members scurry around tying ropes on various floundering Frenchmen and trying to unjam another 'frog', perhaps the world's most perfect fender, who is stuck between the now infamous trimaran and the motor boat.

French Revolution? Well, it *was* a bit like storming the Bastille that day. . .

· · · — — — · · ·

'Hold on to your hat. Here comes another one!'

Frank Wood

British Competitor, The Observer Singlehanded Transatlantic Race 1984

WOOD'S LOG

1032, Monday 4th June. Lat 48°53'. Long 11° 19'

My trimaran, *Marsden*, while doing 12 knots suddenly stops dead in its tracks. I hear banging on the hull and think we must have hit a large wave. Emerging on deck, I see two small whales only 40 feet from the Tri. I'm fascinated – it's the first time I've seen whales at sea. I dive inside for my camera but, by the time I've got it set up, the whales are too far away. The front dagger board has been pulled right out of its casing by the impact and is knocking loudly on the main hull. It was attached to the uphaul line. I quickly take off all sail and begin the laborious task of recovering the dagger board in a Force 6 wind and sea with the aid of a lasso of s/s wire. I recover the board after a colossal struggle taking over three hours.

1344, Monday 4th June

Got sailing again but when I went into the cabin, found it full of water to a depth of nine inches. The force of the dagger board banging has destroyed the Sumlog impeller and sea water is leaking through the damaged fitting. I bail out, tighten up the fitting and continue on my way with a lot of catching up to do – almost four hours lost.

2000, Tuesday 5th June. Lat 45°15'. Long 15°51'

I'm winding the boat up after biding my time for so long. Perfect multihull conditions: 15 to 20 knots of wind – going upwind with one reef in the main and Yankee jib up. Today is the first time I've felt relaxed. Thoroughly enjoying the race and feel that I'm going to do well. I'm well-positioned for some south-westerlies of medium wind when the wind change comes. . .

. . . Dismasted in 20 knots of wind, doing 14 to 16 knots. Mast fell over onto port float; rigging and sails are everywhere. I see a ship on the horizon and call her up on the VHF but get no reply. I realise that I've got no aerial. There's a spare emergency aerial but in my confusion I couldn't remember where I'd put it. By the time I had found it, the ship had gone.

Began the Herculean task of getting the 57 ft mast back on to the boat and recovering rigging and sails. Using my spare tiller as a lever and the boat's winches, I finally got the mast on to the main hull as it was getting dark. I am completely exhausted. I'm going to rest now and tidy up the rigging and sails in the morning. The mast is not bent in any way and there's very little damage.

1200, Wednesday 6th June

Still tired but have almost tidied the boat up as much as possible.

1810, Wednesday 6th June

Have erected the boom and got a bit of sail up. Doing about three knots in a SE direction; 420 miles to Oporto.

1926, Tuesday 12th June
Have been nearly run down by a ship which passed only 100 yards across my stern. I called up on the VHF and asked them to radio Lisbon to give out a 'danger to shipping' alert. Visibility only 200 yards.

0638, Wednesday 13th June
U.S.A. Empire training ship calls me up on the VHF and offers assistance. Says he has me on radar and will close shortly after a Portuguese warship calls me up to ask what the problem is and to take over from the U.S.A. training ship.

'But oh no! You just had to go playing chicken in the shipping lanes again, didn't you?'

0700
Portuguese warship emerges out of the mist. Visibility only 200 yards. Captain comes aboard *Marsden* and is very helpful.

0800
60 miles to Lexios. I am under tow doing 15 knots.

1012
Under orders to slip tow. Lexios tug-boat requires 200,000 escudos for the seven mile tow to Lexios. I bargain hard and get it down to 60,000.

1535
Arrive in Lexios. Greeted by T.V. etc. Clear Customs. Receive permit to sail *Marsden* in Portuguese waters for six months despite having no ship's papers.

Thursday 14th June
Roy from Marsden Building Society, my race sponsor, arrives to give me assistance to get *Marsden* ready for going to sea. He is followed later by Dennis and my wife, Val.

Wednesday 20th June
We have hired a small crane which is really too small but if we wait for low water it should do the job. Everything is going well – the mast is at 45° – when a Maritime Police Launch arrives on the scene causing a lot of swell: what a help! Six police surround our whole operation. Their Chief comes aboard *Marsden* and asks for the ship's papers. I show him the only papers we have – the Plymouth to Newport race instructions and manuals on how to operate the SatNav, VHF and pressure cooker.

He orders me to accompany him immediately to the Police Station with the papers. I bluntly tell him I'm the Ship's Captain and will go with him when the mast is completely secured in the upright position and not before. At this, he asks to take the papers and tells me I should go on later to the Police Station. Again, bluntly, I tell him that the yacht was competing in a race organised by the Royal Western Yacht Club of England and that the Patron is H.R.H. Prince Philip, the Queen's husband. Hearing this, he relents and says I should go to the Police Station in one hour's time and orders me not to try to leave with the boat.

While all this is going on, the tide has risen and this means that the crane is too small for the job. With much difficulty, we manage to secure the mast helped by nearly everyone in the marina.

Accompanied by two policemen, Roy and I are escorted to the Police Station which is over a drawbridge and inside a castle. Here I am questioned:

(1) How many crew were on board, apart from the captain? Answer – nil.
(2) How many engines are aboard? Of what horsepower? Answer – nil.
(3) What is the speed of the vessel? Answer – up to 25 knots.

The papers are taken off me as I try to explain that I was competing in a singlehanded race to Newport, U.S.A., that I didn't mean to sail to Portugal initially and that I was in the 'Queen's race to America when the mast – kaputt.'

The policeman could obviously not read English and was most puzzled by the pressure cooker instructions. I told him that he could not keep the instructions as I would starve, but he not only didn't find this funny, he couldn't even understand.

Eventually, by sign language, he realised what the instructions were and the whole barracks erupted into laughter.

After this, the Commandant said he would be going to London on holiday the following morning and asked whether it would be okay if he called in at Buckingham Palace to have a cup of tea with the Queen.

I assured him that it would be alright as long as he mentioned the name of the yacht, *Marsden*; then he would be most welcome.

He told us that he wanted to hold on to our passports but we replied that we would have to bring them in the morning as we had left them on the boat.

By this time we had been in the castle for nearly two hours and were itching to get going.

Thursday 21st June

We arrived at the castle with our passports at 0900 but no one spoke English, let alone knew what it was all about. Beforehand, we had telephoned the Royal Western Yacht Club in Plymouth and they had advised us not to part with them, so we didn't.

Two weeks later, I returned to the castle with Josie, a Portuguese member of the local yacht club, who asked on my behalf if I could leave as the yacht was ready.

The reply was quite simple: it would not be possible for us to leave until the repairs had been inspected. When asked the earliest moment this could be arranged, the answer was three weeks on Thursday.

Not having the time to hang around much longer, I decided to sail that evening at 0000 hours with a young French boy, called François, who had volunteered to help me sail the boat to Bayona in northern Spain.

We arranged a one-mile tow out to sea with a French yacht who eventually slipped our line at about 0100. Unfortunately there was no wind the whole night and when daylight came we were still one mile from the harbour entrance. Luckily, the visibility was fairly poor – about 400 yards – so we weren't spotted.

After two days of very fluky light winds, we arrived in Bayona. . .

* * *

Looking back, I try to rationalise why I would want to compete in this race again despite what happened in 1984. The only answer I can come up with is:

> To me, life is a challenge to be taken up.
> If it is not taken up, life is just an existence.

. . . — — . . .

The Rt Hon David Steel, M.P.

Leader of the Liberal Party

IMPOLITIC MOVE

I was on holiday last year on a magnificent motor yacht owned by a Greek friend, from which we were able to water ski.

I am a reasonably accomplished water skier but, on this particular occasion, I had a mental aberration and put on the skis before I had finished getting down the ladder into the water – I was therefore stuck halfway down, feet in skis, skis on narrow vertical steps. The result was that I was unable to go up or down or even to fall into the water, and was left with my arms wound round the handrail.

There was no damage done apart from some bruises but, needless to say, this considerable loss of dignity did not go unnoticed by family, friends and crew!

Jonathan Dimbleby

Broadcaster and Journalist

ONLY TOO EASY TO DOOLITTLE

Scene: At Dartmouth, on the river Dart.

Protagonist: Myself, returning from shopping with a boat-load of young children.

Speech: I issue a sharp warning to be careful when clambering down the harbour wall steps into the dinghy.

Extras: A small crowd gathers to watch.

Action: Bearing an armful of magazines and newspapers, I put my foot tentatively into the dinghy. It moves. Suddenly I am in 16 feet of freezing cold water, fully clothed and wearing spectacles. I sink. Eventually I come up for air, with my glasses still on and carrying the sodden newspapers under my arm, trying hard to preserve my tattered dignity.

Extras: Jeers from the crowd. Gleeful comments like: 'You should be on television!'

Protagonist waves genially, feels ridiculous. Children mock him all the cold way home.

Moral: Say unto others. . .

'Ignore them darling, I think we did very well for our first lock!'

Chris Butler

British Competitor, The Observer Singlehanded Transatlantic Race 1980

WHEN THE OIL RUNS OUT. . .

'Eureka,' cried Archimedes as he ran down the streets of Athens, flashing his wares, having discovered the wherefores with which we successfully float upon the ocean.

'Hell!' cried Butler as he detached his body from the sole of the galley having discovered the answer to the world's lubrication problems when the oil runs out.

★　★　★

It is a well-known fact that in 1976 the weather was atrocious for The Observer Singlehanded Transatlantic Race. Less well-known is that the 1984 race suffered weather just as bad at times, but about a week after the big multihulls reached Newport, Rhode Island and therefore that weather has rarely been recorded.

O.S.T.A.R. 1980, however, was more gentle; but there was a stage when I recorded 45 knots of wind and it was during this period that I made my earthquaking discovery.

Achillea was bounding along on a close reach with much reduced area on her cutter rig, at times leaping mid-air off the crest of an advancing wave to crash down into the trough behind it. Well-dressed in my Henri-Lloyds and firmly strapped into the cockpit, I could sit and enjoy the magnificence of the eternity of ranges of small mountains passing under me, lifing *Achillea* up and making holes into which we fell.

Some dolphins came to play tag alongside. To see this display without getting a face-full of green water required careful timing, something I never achieved. I did doubt the dolphins' commonsense in playing around in such bad seas and suggested they would get less wet in calmer waters.

They smiled.

After a longish while I felt cold enough to go down below to make my evening meal, but the movement prevented me from doing my normal Cordon Bleu cooking so I went into my sleeping bag less than well fed. Inevitably, there were sail changes during the night and, next morning, I was determined to have a good breakfast despite the movements of the boat.

First, I ensured that *Achillea* was properly canvassed and going as fast as conditions allowed. Then I removed my oilskins.

Now, the accommodation of *Achillea* is laid out purely for singlehanded racing and the excellent galley is opposite and *en suite* with the equally excellent navigation area. The large chart table is hinged to permit entry into the snug and comfortable seat and rests upon a substantial bracket, but it is unfortunate that under certain circumstances it is possible for one's posterior to lift the chart table when slaving at the galley and to suffer a sharp nip in

40

that fleshy protuberance due to the pincer movement between the underside of the table and the bracket.

Breakfast was to be muesli followed by fried bacon and eggs, crisped together in a deep saucepan from which I also ate. It is quite a pretty saucepan.

Carefully wedged against the chart table, I opened a carton of long-life milk and lodged it in one of the two sinks. One of my virtually unbreakable deep Crewmaster plates was in my left hand and the opened box of Alpen in the other, and I tipped a generous portion of muesli into the plate. The box was successfully stowed away and the carton of milk picked up. Having poured a precise helping of milk on to the muesli, my mouth watered at the vision of this delightful concoction.

A huge wave passed under *Achillea* and, at full speed, she threw herself into the trough behind it. My feet became unstuck; my head bounced against the coachroof. Nevertheless my reactions, alert as ever, directed that I throw the plate and its succulent contents into the nearest sink. I succeeded. But the plate bounced out of the sink, flew through the air spewing my lovely muesli everywhere and smashed itself into many fragments under the chart table. Meanwhile, my after end had lifted the chart table and inserted itself between the jaws of the pincer.

It has been said that I am overweight; I always disagree, saying that the flab is muscle in an embryo state. Embryo muscle or not, all of my weight except for that small part wedged between the chart table and its bracket landed on top of the table and added power to the jaws of the pincer.

It hurt.

I fell free and slithered forward until my legs straddled the base of the mast. That hurt.

I tried to stand. My feet went from beneath me. Every movement was foiled until my hands secured a grip and hauled me up. Still my feet flailed on the cabin sole. Muesli and milk combined to form a perfect lubricant, what is more it transferred miraculously into the cockpit, on to the deck; in fact, everywhere.

Like Archimedes before me, though in a different language, I cried 'Hell!'

It took two days of hard scrubbing to get rid of that muesli while the gale still raged. After that came two days of calm.

I missed that breakfast – but discovered a never-ending supply of lubricant. The world should be proud of me.

Archimedes would!

'This is the spot. They come ready peeled here!'

Sir Peter Tennant

Retired Don, Past Diplomat and Businessman

SEAL OF CONFESSION

I used to sail and fish with two Swedish fishermen in the Baltic between Sweden and Finland. They lived on the island of Möja in the Stockholm archipelago and I often called in on them to buy some of their fresh smoked Baltic herring (strömming) and drink a 'kaffe kask' (coffee and schnaps) and talk about life.

The archipelago was full of interesting people – smugglers, artists, fishermen and seal-hunters. Even in those days there was an old bearded seal-hunter dressed in furs with a long spear who made a living from seal-hunting mostly in the spring when the seals moved south with the break-up of the ice in the Gulf of Bothnia. Occasionally we met up with seals with their young in the outer archipelago but they kept well away from the angry fishermen who killed them for spoiling their nets.

My friends, Oscar and Petrus, agreed to come out with me to Gillöga, a little cluster of rocks well out to sea, where they had a hut and caught a variety of fish including pike. They said the seals were on the move and they would help me get one. So I took my gun and we manoeuvred my boat into a cove near the hut where there was a look-out point masked by an old mine recovered from World War I.

We fished and cooked and drank and sang well into the night and I then went on board and fell into a deep sleep. At about 4 a.m. my companions woke me and dragged me up to the old mine. From there they pointed to some rocks half a mile away and said if I looked hard I would see a seal. We tumbled into a rowing boat, muffled the oars and approached the island up wind. As we got nearer the seal disappeared below the crest of the rise and I was prompted to crawl up the rocks within sight and range.

I made my approach in exemplary silence and then slowly raising my head I saw my prey and fired. It fell over and I got up to collect my first seal.

There was a burst of jeers and laughter. Oscar and Petrus could not contain themselves at my discomposure.

The seal was not a seal at all. It was the carcass of a pig washed ashore from a passing coaster which they had rigged up with the greatest artistry.

That cured me of seal-hunting for ever. The story got round the archipelago and for years I was known as the English Pig-hunter.

· · · — — · · ·

Peter Porter

Architect

THE NEW HAND

We had arranged to pick him up on the pontoon at Lymington for the Sunday morning Winter Series race. He lived with a neighbour's daughter and, for ages, had been badgering me to get on the boat and do some racing with us. He'd got plenty of experience, he said. Done some R.O.R.C. racing and more down in the West Country. An all-round hand, could navigate a bit and had had to helm and skipper a couple of times in bad storms when everyone else was ill.

He was waiting for us on the end of a long pontoon which had just enough space for my thirty-five footer. We were going to moor on the starboard side, fenders were out and forward and stern lines were ready. There were two of us on board as the rest of the crew had also arranged to join us in Lymington.

I sent my girlfriend forward and told her to pass him the line, then come back, step ashore and tie up aft. I'd judged the manoeuvre more or less perfectly and sidled up nicely to the pontoon. He received the forward line neatly, pulled on it as hard as he could and wrapped it round the first cleat. The boat's nose went straight into the pontoon and we spun round, hitting it with our unfendered port side, and narrowly missed the next boat. Morning, he said. Right on time. I was not sure what to say – perhaps I'd been doing it wrong all these years or had not explained my strategy properly. I shut up.

From the start, the race was a beat. I sent him up with my normal foredeck pair to get the spinnaker ready for the first mark. We were nicely in the middle of the pack. We turned and up she went. But a lazy halyard had not been brought back and the sail went up between that and the forestay, wrapping round it nicely. They were getting in a right state up at the bow and, in the end, I put my girlfriend on the helm, told them to get out of the way, and got it down and up again properly.

By then we were last by quite a bit, but only ailing – no damage done. My normal foredeck mumbled something, looking thoroughly ashamed *He*, of course, said nothing. I was beginning to worry. There was a stiff breeze and my kite is huge. There was a mark ahead and we had to get the thing down somehow. Coming up to the mark, I assigned the crew their jobs. I put *him* on the uphaul: I didn't think he could do much harm there.

Do it slow, I said. We'll pass the mark, run, gybe, and then get on our new course. Nothing clever; text-book stuff. The foredeck called for the pole. *He* let the uphaul go completely. It crashed down, nearly taking the foredeck's arm with it, and was over the side in the water. We slewed round and all hell broke loose. I don't believe her, but my girlfriend said I was shouting and swearing. I *know* I was calmly giving instructions.

We had to winch the pole out of the water. It had never happened to me before and I was amazed at the power of the water and the difficulty we had

'Quit larking about and get the damned thing down!'

getting it out. We did, finally gybed, and got on course. All the other boats had vanished.

I now started worrying about getting it down. Where could I send *him*? Hell, let what happens happen! It did. Straight over the side. Under the boat. Everything. He'd pulled on the other corner, nearly putting everyone over the side. We got it back, amazingly still in one piece.

The other boats were on the second lap. We're going into the bar for a pint, I said. We moored and he was unhanking the jib. Leave it on, I said, we need it for going back.

I sat in the corner of the bar with my girlfriend; the crew were keeping well away. He came up and said: Well, that wasn't too bad for the first time out together. I don't remember my reply.

We had a couple of pints and I said to the crew: Let's take her home. Some of them were coming back with us to Beaulieu. The foredeck put the halyard on the jib and came back to wind it up. Something was wrong. For Heaven's sake, stop messing around and do something properly for a change, I said. Well, even I was surprised to find *he'd* hanked it back on upside down!

. . . ——— . . .

Roddy Llewellyn

Landscape Architect and Author

BUZZING AROUND

My mother used to keep bees. When she was eight months pregnant with me she was attacked by her swarm and stung all over, having been chased round the house several times.

As a result I have always been terrified of bees (and wasps) but there is an old wives' tale which says that if you have been stung several times by bees you develop 'green fingers'. Obviously my love of plants was instilled into me when still in the embryo!

You may be wondering what on earth this has to do with sailing. Well, when I was on holiday in Turkey one year, I took out a small sailing boat to visit a tiny island off the coast. The water was calm but I did have oars to help me on my way.

When I got within 200 yards of the island, a swarm of bees engulfed me. I was so frightened that I froze and could not move an inch. They were everywhere – in my hair and all over my body.

Very slowly, I turned the boat round using one oar and *very* gently rowed back towards the mainland. One by one, the bees detached themselves and flew home. Extraordinarily enough, I was not stung once, much to my relief.

It was only later that I discovered that the offshore island was owned by a monastic order self-sufficient in food – and especially, no doubt, honey!

. . . ——— . . .

'Now we know why they call it Beehive Island.'

Air Marshal Sir John Curtiss,

K.C.B., K.B.E.

Director, The Society of British Aerospace Companies Ltd

A NIGHT'S CACOPHONY

Most anecdotes connected with the sea, humorous or otherwise, centre around the wind, weather and other yachtsmen's behaviour at sea. Mine concerns problems when safely tied up alongside because, even under such normally safe and incontrovertible circumstances, everything is not plain sailing.

My tale concerns a weekend cruise undertaken some seven years ago by a crew of twelve – nine men and three girls – in a Nicholson 55. We left Portsmouth/Gosport in the afternoon and, after dividing everyone into two watches with the skipper and cook (one of the girls) on call as required, we sailed through the night to Cherbourg – our first stop for stores and duty-free. We were away from there by midday and, after a short but exhilarating sail, were safely tied up alongside the mole in Alderney harbour. There we were to spend the night in comparative comfort for, with the sails stowed on deck, there is a bunk for everyone in a boat that size.

The evening started with an enjoyable run ashore, an excellent meal and more than a few drinks. Just as well, since by the time we returned to the boat the tide was out and it looked a very long drop down on a rust-eaten iron ladder to the deck. Gallantly operating on the principle of ladies first – 'They'll be soft to fall on,' remarked one of our number – we were soon safely aboard but in need of further refreshment to still our nerves.

We then played a series of childishly noisy but enjoyable card games before turning in for the night and some well-earned rest – or so I thought. With a four on, four off watch system the night before, we were all pretty tired and ready for sleep. But I had reckoned without the combined efforts of well-wined, dined and overtired companions. No, to be fair, I cannot claim to have distinguished for certain that any of the ladies actually snored but, by God, the eight men made up for any shortfall on their part!

What was almost uncanny was that there was no build-up to this unearthly chorus. The cabin lights were doused, perhaps a minute or two passed, and then, as if some invisible conductor had raised a baton, the whole boat reverberated into one unholy monumental snore. No, that is not quite right. It was eleven or maybe eight wholly unco-ordinated, untuned but individual snores. They had clearly never rehearsed and they had no volume control; it was full volume from the start.

Anyone who has never experienced the full-throated – or should it be 'nasaled' – impact of a battery of snores all unleashing their sound within the confines of a boat's cabin can have not the slightest idea of the effect on a lone non-sleeper.

There was no hope of sleep while that noise continued. For while one can cope with a single snore by shouting or throwing something (preferably heavy), faced by up to eleven the task is impossible.

Shouting made no difference at all, unless it was a slight change of key; throwing a sea boot on the cabin deck even less. So after enduring some fifteen minutes of this row, which at no time showed the least signs of diminishing in volume nor for that matter any improvement in harmony, I noisily left the cabin with my sleeping bag for the well deck where, despite a slight drizzle, I slept comparatively peacefully.

All of my companions expressed surprise and disbelief the next morning that any of them, let alone *all*, had been snoring. As the ladies took the same line, I can only say that I, ungallantly perhaps, conclude that they were as guilty as my males colleagues.

That was the last time I spent the night with eleven others in one cabin and time has by no means lessened the memory or the determination never to repeat the experience.

Does snoring render one deaf, I wonder? How else did my companions manage to sleep?

. . . ——— . . .

Sir John Mills, C.B.E.

Actor, Producer and Director

TOTTING UP THE ODDS

In those early days of filming I always insisted that whenever possible I should be allowed to do my own stunts. Fire I was not keen on, but with anything else I was always ready to have a go.

Puffin (as Asquith was known to his friends – he looked very like one) described a shot that he said would be very effective without the use of a double. During a lunch break he took me up to the top deck of the cruiser we were shooting on at sea and showed me the plan of action. The scene was to be shot at night. It entailed Able Seaman Brown's escaping from the German cruiser. The camera would pick me up creeping through a cabin door, rifle in hand, boots tied round my neck; then, when no crew were in sight, I was to cross the deck, climb the rail, drop overboard into the sea and start the swim to Resolution Island. The point was, Puffin explained, that as it would be one continuous shot with no cuts, the audience would know that no double had been used and it would therefore have much more reality.

The day was warm and sunny. I had a look over the rails. A long drop, I thought, but not too desperate. I was a strong swimmer and confident that I could make it. 'Right, Puffin,' I said. 'No problem. It's a great shot.'

The call was for 8.30 p.m. the following evening. I arrived at the ship in a whaler at 7.30 p.m., changed in the mess and at eight o'clock made my way to the top deck. The weather was appalling, bitterly cold with a damp sea mist. Puffin was huddled up in a duffle coat. 'Hallo, Johnnie, it's a lousy night, but exactly what we want for the scene.'

'I want to get this in one take, so try and look really *terrified as you plummet to your doom.'*

The ship looked ghostly in the arc-light. 'Let's just walk through it several times. It's a tricky shot for the focus-puller. We've plenty of time, and we have to get this in Take One – for your sake. Props, get Johnnie a duffle coat – it's freezing.'

I walked to the ship's rail and looked down. At what seemed like a hundred feet below, a small collection of rowing boats manned by sailors were floating in a large circle in the sea. Each boat contained lifebelts and coils of rope. The floodlights cast eerie shadows on the oily water.

A voice beside me said, 'It looks worse at night, doesn't it? They've got the boats down there. If anything goes wrong they'll fish you out in a flash. But it will be great if, when you surface, you could manage to swim away from the ship until you're out of the lights.' Puffin paused and looked sideways at me. 'Sure you don't want a double for the jump? I could cut the shot when you get to the ship's rail, you know.'

The temptation was enormous to chicken out, but it would have required more courage than the actual jump. 'No problem,' I said. 'Why lose one of the best shots in the picture?'

We walked it through several times and, as there was still fifteen minutes to go until zero hour Puffin suggested that I waited in one of the cabins out of the wind. I was sitting staring out of the porthole wondering if I had renewed my life insurance policy when the door opened and a Petty Officer appeared.

'Scuse me, sir,' he said, 'but I hear you're going in the drink tonight, and as it's a bit on the nippy side, we thought you might like to pop into our mess and have a small tot to keep out the cold.'

'That is the happiest thought you've had for years,' I said. 'Lead me to it.'

The small tot turned out to be half a tumbler of that marvellous, oily, amber-coloured liquid called Navy Rum. In a few minutes I was a new man. That tot really hit the jackpot. The effect on an empty stomach was electric – courage spurted from every pore. Then the second assistant came to tell me that they would not be ready for another half an hour – camera problem.

'Time for the other half, sir?'

'Thank you, Petty Officer, why not? Best drink I've ever had in my life.'

Twenty minutes later, when they were ready to shoot, Able Seaman Albert Brown was happily smashed and willing, if asked, to jump off the Eiffel Tower with no safety net. I made my way with great care and precision to the deck where the wardrobe department undid my boots, tied the laces together and hung them round my neck; a rifle was put into my hand.

Puffin arrived. 'We're all set,' he said. 'How're you feeling?'

'Terrific. Abs'lutely trific.'

Puffin gave me a rather old-fashioned look and took half a step backwards. Navy Rum is lethal up to four feet. 'All right, Johnnie, let's shoot it. I'm using a wide-angled lens so if you don't hit all the marks on the way to the rail it won't matter. Take your time there. Look right and left before you jump. I want to make certain the audience will know it's you and not a double.'

Action. I opened the cabin door and crept slowly, bent double, across the deck. If the scene had necessitated walking upright in a straight line I couldn't have made it. I reached the rail, climbed it, looked right and left as directed and then down at the water. By the light of the arc-lamps I could see the rescue boats bobbing about on the fringe of the circle. The drop looked horrific. Taking a deep breath and mentally crossing myself, I jumped. During the fall, which seemed endless, headlines flashed through my mind: 'Gallant young actor drowned'; 'John Mills, rising young star, extinguished.' I hit the water, which felt like concrete, and disappeared into the icy depths.

After a struggle I surfaced and, still grasping the rifle, struck out away from the ship. Once out of the floodlit area hands grabbed me and I was hauled on board on to the rowing boats. Take One was OK. Everything worked. It was a print. Puffin was delighted and so was I. By this time I was sober, and in that condition nothing in the world could have persuaded me to give a repeat performance.

From *Up In The Clouds, Gentlemen Please* by Sir John Mills (George Weidenfeld & Nicolson Ltd)

· · · — — — · · ·

The Duke of Northumberland,

K.G., G.C.V.O.

Treasurer, Royal National Lifeboat Institution

TRANSPORT OF DELIGHT

I have only once been sailing, many years ago, with a friend who had a 40 ft Bermudan ketch. Owing to some miscalculation entering the Crinan Canal we failed to stop. The bowsprit went straight through the lock gates and the canal began to empty.

This caused considerable consternation as the then Minister of Transport was coming to inspect the canal the following morning. I was told that it was to be the first visit by a V.I.P. since Queen Victoria opened it!

Considering the portfolio of the Minister in question, I have always felt subsequently that it was rather bad timing for our 'gaffe'.

. . . ——— . .

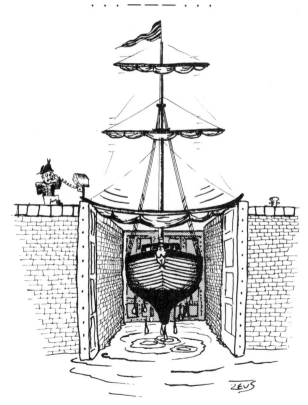

'Isambard, it's Horatio here. Remember those dimensions I gave you for the new lock?'

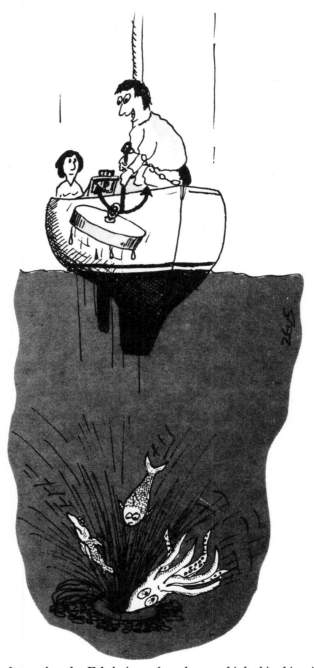

'Well for heaven's sake Ethel, just what do you think this thing is?'

Sue Arnold

Journalist

PARADISE LOST

It was a perfect summer's evening for a sail. We were on a flotilla holiday in Yugoslavia – the first and only time I've ever been afloat. As agreed with our lead-boat, we were nosing in to a tranquil bay near Trogir. Actually, we cheated a bit and switched on the engine to make sure we got there without a hitch.

Only one other boat was idling in this idyllic bay. It was German. The couple on board had picked a secluded spot to anchor and obviously thought the place was theirs for the night. On our approach they appeared on deck, stark naked, shouting at us to go away. We tried hard to make ourselves understood in our non-existent German, warning them that the bay was a pre-planned rendezvous for the twelve yachts in our flotilla. It was useless. Despite frantic arm-waving and roaring, the stitch-less German skipper (I don't think they *ever* carry clothes on board although he *was* sporting a rather smart blue yachting cap) could not make us budge. Literally. Because, by this time, not only were the twelve boats bearing sixty-five English yachties in noisy, jolly holiday mood arriving one by one, but our anchor line had wrapped itself round theirs and the two boats were now inextricably entangled. It was absolute chaos.

The skipper in the lead-boat had already decided that the bay would be a blissful spot for a barbecue, so the sixty-five English holiday-makers, including us, spent the entire evening eating, getting drunk, dancing and singing at the tops of our voices on the rocks.

Coupled so lovingly with our boat, there was nothing the German pair could do except wait until morning when we untangled the anchor line and made off.

So I suppose it just goes to show that when you think you're in paradise, it can only too quickly turn out to be hell after all!

· · · — — — · · ·

Paul Eddington

Actor

NOT ALWAYS BLARNEY

About a quarter of a century ago, I went with some friends to Kilkeel in Northern Ireland to buy a boat and sail it back down to Dun Laogharie.

We set out on a fine morning only to be met by fishing boats coming in the other direction who all shouted to us: 'Go home.'

I need hardly explain that my friends and I are not ourselves sailors when I tell you that we were puzzled, but not unduly alarmed, by this.

We continued on our journey and very soon a Force 8 gale blew up – not an experience I wish to encounter again in an open boat. Eventually, we managed to go about and barely achieved the return to Kilkeel. Unfortunately, no one noticed our return and we learned later that the entire Irish coast had been on the look-out for us.

A sobering tale and one which, I think, has a moral.

. . . —— — . . .

' "Fishermen" you said, "fearmongers" you said, "always predict bad weather" you said, "don't listen to them" you said.'

Margery Hurst, O.B.E.

Joint Chairman, Brook Street Bureau of Mayfair Ltd

BETTER LATE THAN NEVER

The greatest risk in my sailing career was the nearness of my having missed it altogether. I came to sailing late, having thought myself inoculated against the bug by excessive early exposure.

After this, other problems interposed themselves and I had moved inland. My circle no longer shared my background. 'What? Go sailing?' said those few to whom I confessed that I harboured that ambition. 'Go sailing and spend your weekends soaking wet, dining on soggy cereal, sick to your stomach, and sixty quid the poorer for it – or worse still, perhaps, vegetating in some ghastly waterfront pub waiting for the wind to change.'

'Forget it,' they said, embellishing on the much-quoted royal remark: 'If you like standing under a cold shower tearing up five pound notes, you'll love sailing.'

But I couldn't forget it – a Portsmouth girl, I'd first seen sails from the safety of my pram, learned to regard the sea as part of the garden, the Navy as a section of nursery school and later, in the company of young midshipmen, to discover that a cool hand with a boat was as fine a Lochinvar as any adept at the tango.

Half a lifetime later, the desire to fly across the waves, canvas above and fishy seas below, reasserted itself. I confided the wish to my husband who embraced it wholeheartedly and made the project quite his own.

The outcome of that episode was *Lady Galadriel*. Not exactly the creature of the wind I had envisaged, *Lady Galadriel* was too large for my dreams and pleased my husband much more than she pleased me.

But in the end I made it: a Moody 32, later to be upgraded to a Moody 39.

Midgie 11 and I have not attended at any ocean rescues nor have we survived any particularly terrifying terrors of the deep by the skin of our teeth. Instead we have survived the minor crises of wall-to-wall eggs in the galley and tangled rigging at major regattas.

We have lived to enjoy the knowledge that if we desist from polluting the air with diesel fumes the wind will be kind and waft us across the water like a gull – provided, of course, that we bend our understanding to her moods and remember that sailing is something we humans do because, like Everest to Hillary, the wind and sea are there.

· · · — — · · ·

David Duncombe

British Competitor, The Observer Singlehanded Transatlantic Race 1984

WHALE OF A TIME

The Observer Singlehanded Transatlantic Race is, in my view, the perfect yacht race, requiring dedication and determination just to get to the starting line. It follows a course across 3000 miles of windy, iceberg-strewn ocean and just to finish would prove to me that I wasn't the 'wally' many said I was.

At 0230 hours the alarm rang, but I was already awake. Something was wrong but I didn't know what. The wind was strong from the north-west and the boat was moving fast although well heeled over to port. The weather was clear and I needed it to remain that way. Having had gales and rain for days, I wasn't at all sure where I was and needed a few sun sights to fix my position, which should have been somewhere well to the north of the Azores.

From where I was sitting in the companionway hatch there was nothing in sight, just the endless train of breaking wave crests.

Quite without warning and with a sickening crunch, the keel struck a submerged object and the boat stopped dead – so completely that the bows dipped under, shipping hundreds of gallons of green sea. As if in slow motion, a mini-tidal wave swept backwards along the deck before striking me in the chest and sloshing below to saturate charts, books, bedding . . . everything.

My initial reaction was that I had struck rocks and that I was aground and therefore miles out on my navigation. Then I saw it. Covered in phosphorescent sparks and rising slowly from the water, right there, right by the side of my boat, were the flukes and tail of a whale, so big that they seemed to blot out everything. With no apparent effort, the tail smashed into the hull and deck, ripping lifelines and stanchions out, backing plates and all, leaving great gaping holes everywhere.

All I could do was gape and stare. The animal surfaced completely, blowing as he did so and giving a whole new meaning to the word 'halitosis', to lie in the water watching me as the waves crashed over his back.

That was surely my worst moment and was when I wished that I had taken up knitting instead because I was certain that he was about to turn and ram me. However, after what seemed an age but probably wasn't more than a minute or so, he swam off in the other direction. Never have I known such terror.

After a while I was able to move and make some attempt to repair the boat. She had obligingly tacked herself and was lying hove-to but taking in water through the holes at an alarming rate.

The decision to turn back was an easy one and with the wind now behind me I was able to plug the gaps with cushions, sails, and miles of tape; certainly not repairs, but sufficient to help me limp back to Plymouth.

. . . — — . . .

59

Tony Adams

Actor

LOST ERA

I had bought *Seaway* and taken two years restoring her to days of former glory, ridding her of all attempts at modernisation – strip lighting, polystyrene tiles and pink and blue wallpaper.

Below, she eventually looked like a Pullman railway carriage again and on deck her newly-painted funnel gleamed cream and black – Victorian elegant – an era to which my mother belonged. Mother had written several books under her maiden name of Winifred Brown, and can be found in *Who's Who in Yachting* – a formidable lady who believes firmly in tradition at sea.

I was keeping *Seaway* up the Lymington river and proposed that we should motor to Cowes for lunch. As we got out of the river, Mother suggested we put up *Seaway's* tan-coloured sails which I had just made for her.

'Darling,' I said, 'they're steadying sails. *Seaway* won't actually sail, you know.'

'Nonsense,' came the reply. So I stopped *Seaway's* engines and got out the sails which I kept in the funnel (where else does one keep sails?), and bent them on.

We lolled about in a Force 1 to 3. 'We're going backwards,' I said.

Mother took a green paper from one of her roll-ups, dropped it over the side and growled, 'We're doing half a knot.'

At this point, unbeknown to me, *Seaway*, who is always being admired from afar, was being watched. There was a roar of outboard engines as the inshore lifeboat came to what must have looked like the rescue. And only after giving firm assurances that we hadn't got engine failure and were, in fact, out for a leisurely sail, did they leave alone our Victorian-looking steam yacht with the Victorian lady and that daft actor from television's *Crossroads* aboard!

· · · — — — · · ·

Jimmy Hill

Broadcaster

PIPPED TO THE POST

I am not a sailor and I cannot sail – but I can row and also start an outboard motor, provided that it's this year's model.

On the occasions when I have not been able to start the outboard motor which I used to own, I have sweated profusely, cursed furiously and made up my mind to become a wind-only sailor.

When the outboard motor and the inflatable to which it was attached was stolen from under my nose in Spain last year I imagined that I was at the start of a mercurial sailing career. Unfortunately, before that could happen, my son bought a new engine and attached it to a posh-looking fibreglass job.

So, like the Rodgers and Hart song, now I'm not only a ship without a sail, I'm no longer even inflatable. . .

. . . —— . . .

Admiral Sir Derek Empson,

G.B.E., K.C.B.

Retired Naval Officer and Company Consultant

STERN WARNING

My enthusiasm for sailing was stifled at an early stage – which is perhaps not surprising since my first experience was in an open boat in mid-Atlantic after being sunk by a U-boat in 1941. As a result, I have no humorous sailing anecdotes to relate, only a brief account of the incident which was responsible for this sad state of affairs and in which there were elements of black comedy as well as tragedy – a tragedy that would have been total but for a miracle.

I was one of a number of young naval people taking passage in the S.S. *City of Nagpur* bound for the Indian Ocean where I was to join H.M.S. *Hermes*. Also among the passengers were wives, children and fiancées of army officers serving in India.

We were too slow, at 12 knots, to join a convoy and the plan was therefore to head out from the Clyde to the north-west until beyond the operating range of U-boats and then turn south. Feeling naked and very much alert, we steamed for three or four days until the evening when the Captain announced that we were out of the U-boat range. Not unnaturally we celebrated and when we finally went to our bunks we did so in a very relaxed and happy mood.

At two o'clock in the morning there were four thunderous explosions caused, as it transpired, by four torpedoes from a U-boat which, most unfairly, was operating beyond its range.

There was a certain grim humour in this and in the way the Lascar crew were so well prepared that they were first by a long way into the boats – with all their luggage! But there was nothing amusing in the death of thirteen people, even though this number was unbelievably low in the circumstances, or in the fact that the Captain insisted on remaining on board when the U-boat completed the sinking by gunfire after the boats were clear.

To cut a long story short, we set sail eastwards in our open boats and in a very heavy swell, more in hope than expectation, when – by a miracle – we were spotted by an aircraft being ferried across the Atlantic which, for no apparent reason, descended below the cloud just above us and saw the flares we fired. But for this we would almost certainly still be in mid-Atlantic – at the bottom of it. Instead, we were eventually rescued by a destroyer which was just about to give up the search when she found us.

Sailing was never really the same again for me.

. . . — — — . . .

'I think there may be subs around, Skipper.'

Prue Leith

Restaurateur, Journalist and Broadcaster

VIEW FROM A GALLEY

My only sailing disaster story and, indeed, my only sailing story at all, is of being invited to Cowes for the weekend by Sir Max Aitken. I saw myself in fetching gear, waving to the cameras from the bonnet – oops, I mean bulkhead or deck or something. In fact I spent four miserable hours being sick.

But I did get to see a Prime Minister in bed.

Max, deciding I was more qualified as cook than sailor, ordered me to drum up fellow-guest Ted Heath's breakfast.

'What will you have, P.M.?' says he, expansively.

As decisive as always, Mr Heath replied firmly, 'Half a grapefruit, a 4½ minute egg and a piece of toast.'

Ever tried to find a grapefruit at midnight when you are not quite sober? I must have woken half the island, but the P.M. got his brekker. And I gave up sailing.

'This is the life, eh?'

Colonel W.H. Whitbread

Past Chairman of Whitbread Brewery

BEAST OF CHASE

It was our habit to sail *Lone Fox* to the yard where she was to be laid up for the winter from her summer base at Badachro in Wester Ross during the first week in September. That particular week fitted in well with my chairmanship of the A.G.M. in London which, in those days, fell around September 10th.

However, that year, what had been planned as a leisurely cruise around Skye, Mull and some of the Inner Hebrides went awry when Hurricane Betsy presumably lost her way and landed up on the west coast of Scotland.

We were heading for Fort William with the idea of leaving *Lone Fox* there briefly, while I went south, and then taking her through the Caledonian Canal to Inverness for the winter. A lazy, happy day had been spent, with a short sunny sail in the morning and the afternoon exploring Canna. The island seemed to provide a peaceful anchorage and it was a lovely evening with clear skies and terns diving all around the boat.

At five-thirty the following morning, it wasn't at all like that. Clutching egg-and-bacon sandwiches, we were running through an ominous dark grey sea and gathering murk to Rhum which seemed to provide the nearest and best shelter for *Lone Fox*'s high masts. It was terribly cold.

We passed a noisy and frightening day. *Lone Fox* tore about on a taut anchor chain, the strain zinging through the rigging alarmingly until the electric anchor winch gave up the ghost. This was a serious problem with so much heavy chain out – but one nevertheless had to sympathise with it!

My deadline, the A.G.M. in London, was now only 48 hours away. I tried to contact the brewery to explain our predicament from a call-box which bore the classic number 'Rhum 1'. And a pretty wet, cold, and not to say dicey little expedition to the telephone it proved to be, what with winds, choppy seas and an awfully wet rubber dinghy.

We broke cover at some ghastly hour the following morning with the prospect of a very long and rough sail against time if I was to catch my train. Outside, we met with a good Force 5 or 6, reasonable visibility but colossal seas. We piled on what sails we dared, corkscrewed our way through a vile swell off Ardnamurchan and roared down the Sound of Mull. Unforgettable light relief was provided on board by Sir Jock Brook who regaled us with positively purple stories of scandal and intrigue as we passed various west coast estates and houses. It was hard work, exhilarating and fun.

As we turned north-east into Loch Linnhe we found, inevitably, the wind slap on the nose. Time was definitely running out. *Lone Fox* clawed her way up that loch with helmsmanship worthy of an Admiral's Cup contender.

In those days the Corran Ferry, halfway up Loch Linnhe, was on a chain. The channel is also very narrow. A strong gust hit us from Loch Etive as we entered with rather too much sail up and no room to manoeuvre a boat of *Lone*

'Just made it!'

Fox's size: it was spectacular to say the least. Rail and deck under, we roared through. As we hung on for dear life it was noticed that we had caused considerable disturbance and a goodly traffic jam on shore. One man even threw his hat in the air – one assumes intentionally!

We made it to the entrance of the canal at about 5.30 p.m. with myself at the wheel wearing a City suit beneath my oilies. My secretary and I leaped ashore and into a waiting taxi, bent on catching the sleeper train as it came south from Inverness. The taxi took us half a mile and promptly broke down. We hitched a lift, in the end, on a lorry and arrived at Dalwhinnie ahead of the train and in time to have mixed – and to drink – a Martini of such excellence that it has gone down in family folklore.

We also made the A.G.M. with about an hour to spare. . .

Colonel J.N. Blashford-Snell,

M.B.E., F.R.S.G.S.

Deputy Chairman, Operation Raleigh

ZAIRE RIVER EXPEDITION, 1974.

With sixty porters beneath each huge inflatable boat, we moved them like giant caterpillars down a 1000 foot slope to the river. Here we joined up with the Avon dinghies that had been portaged or controlled by lines through the surging white water towards us. Now only the rapids barred our way to the sea, but with up to 16 million gallons per second pouring through a gorge which had narrowed the Zaïre River to a bare 400 yards, the power can be imagined. Indeed, the depth here was probably about 140 feet at high water. The river seemed to be alive, with great boiling bubbles rushing up from the depths and erupting on the surface. Then, as quickly as they came, they were replaced by whirlpools and swirling currents.

Our porters, many of them Angolan refugees and some almost certainly Freedom Fighters, came with gifts of sugar cane, wine and fruit to see us off. But the river was not going to let us get away unscathed yet.

In the final rapid *La Vision*, my great doughnut-shaped rubber flagship, was momentarily trapped in a whirlpool, like a cork in a wash-tub, being bent downwards and spun round and round with engines screaming.

Before I could stop them coming down, Captain Alun Davies' Avon was capsized by a 15 foot wave. The upturned boat with its crew of three clinging to it was swept towards a yawning whirlpool. The jets at this point had been sent back to Kinshasa and from where I was situated, 1000 yards downriver, I couldn't see what had happened. However, the following 'recce' boat saw the accident and its skipper, Neil Rickards, a Royal Marines corporal, decided to have a go.

Taking his own small craft through the mountains of tossing water, he managed to get right into the whirlpool and circle around inside it, rather like

'It says here "Before you attempt a tricky manoeuvre, turn the engine off, drop the anchor, and think the whole thing through" . . . turn the engine off, George!'

a motorcyclist in a 'wall of death' at a fairground. In the centre of this swirling mass he could see Alun's capsized Avon with its crew of three still clinging on frantically to the lifeline. Eventually, by going the same way that the water was revolving, Neil managed to get his craft alongside the stricken boat so that Bob Powell and Somue, one of the Zaïre Liaison Officers, could pull the three men to safety. Then he circled up again in the same direction that the water was turning and out of the top.

As they left, he looked back and was just in time to see the upturned craft disappear down the vortex.

Downriver, I was surprised a few moments later when the capsized boat bobbed up from the river-bed beside me. The engine was smashed to pieces, the floorboards wrecked and there appeared to be no survivors. But the crew had all been saved, thanks to Neil's courage and skill, for which he was later awarded the Queen's Gallantry Medal and made one of Britain's 'Men of the Year'.

Two days later we reached the little seaport of Banana and at dusk our strange fleet, which had set out almost four months before in the centre of Africa, sailed into the setting sun. Basil, in cassock and surplice, held an improvised cross and beneath the flags of the nations represented in our team he conducted a simple service. Under our hulls, the water heaved gently. Strangely, it no longer tugged and pulled at us; there was no current, for we were now in the Atlantic.

From *A Taste for Adventure* by Colonel J.N. Blashford-Snell (Hutchinson Publishing Group Ltd)

. . . — — — . . .

Dr Magnus Pyke, O.B.E.

Scientist, Author and Broadcaster

LOSER WINS ALL

It was in 1936 that I won the Doreen Cup singlehanded. The Scarab was 16 ft long and could never have been described as fast. But she was comfortable, rigged with roller reefing and tan sails. A garden fork was left forward for digging worms for bait and a crate of beer aft to ameliorate the time spent waiting for a bite.

On the day of the race, I fixed on the outboard and motored to a convenient position well behind the starting line, dropped anchor, unrigged the outboard and settled down with sandwiches and beer to wait for the tide to rise. In due course, the starting gun boomed out. I pulled up the anchor and, with the rest of the fleet, drifted up the river.

It was a flat calm. When the tide turned, we all drifted back again. After handicaps had been computed, it was announced that I had won. Thereafter, the beautiful Irish-silver trophy graced my mantelpiece.

The winner the previous year had been a certain Miss Vaughan with her darling, narrow-gutted *Betsy*. She was soon to see the Doreen Cup leave *her* mantelpiece.

She got it back though. She married me.

Patrick Mower

Actor

KIRK'S TEETH

The glint on Kirk Douglas's clenched teeth could be seen beaming its way through the sparkling sea spray as he opened the throttle of his outboard motor to its full extent. His rubber dinghy ploughed into the nose of mine. I did a Nureyev somersault twelve feet into the air and plunged with a Cadbury's Milk Tray dive into the freezing sea loch. The hero had given the villain his come-uppance.

That was the scene the public saw in the film *Catch Me A Spy*. In real life the pirouetting chocolate deliverer was in fact a stunt man; and although Kirk's teeth were his own, most of the action wasn't. He also had a double for this innocent stunt that proved to be extremely dangerous.

In order to get close-up shots of me for the 'chase sequence' Frank, an amiable 6 ft 7 in bearded Goliath of a camera operator, had to squeeze himself and his camera into the front of my 8 ft dinghy. The story called for a reaction shot of my horror as I realise that Kirk Douglas's boat is on a collision course with mine.

The stunt man doubling for Mr Douglas proved to be over-zealous. Instead of nudging the side of my boat we had a head-on collision, both doing 30 m.p.h. Frank was ten feet in the air when he decided to let go of the camera which hurtled past my right ear two seconds before he hurtled past my left.

The upside down boat followed next, and by some miracle of physics (maybe the air trapped between the water's surface and the boat combined with my instinctive kick as I went backwards into the loch) I found myself sitting in the righted boat. Frank, however, was not so lucky. I pulled the floundering giant to the side of the boat to be greeted by:

'Pat, my waders! They're filling up with water!'

He then slowly sank below the surface. Grabbing him by both hair and beard, I managed to pull his head above the water and I yelled:

'Breathe!' – which he managed to do before I had to lower his 18 stone plus mass back in the water to give my screaming arms a rest.

I repeated this operation for what seemed like an age, lifting and lowering, until the stunt man had managed to start his engine and reach us. It took the two of us twenty-five minutes to haul the sodden man and his saturated waders back on board.

So when you see it on the silver screen, please remember the villain was really . . . the hero.

. . . — — . . .

'He says he wants a stand-in for the next shot.'

John Ridgway, M.B.E.

Round-the-World Yachtsman and Director, John Ridgway School of Adventure

PICKING UP THE MOORING

Early spring, just south of Cape Wrath. The dry south-east wind had poured off the shore all day, keeping the sea flat and progress brisk.

I was bringing a course of adults back to the John Ridgway School of Adventure. They were looking forward to their supper – the lunchtime walk round Handa Island seemed long gone.

We'd got on pretty well together. Ivor was the catalyst – portly, flat check cap and aggressive specs – he was the very model of the modern Midas from the Midlands. His stories and humour had astonished a quiet pair of doctors from Aberdeen but other, more grainy chaps looked a little doubtful. When the time came to select a daring fellow to jump into the rubber dinghy on the mooring, there was only one choice: the crew were unanimously for Ivor.

We were moving fast on a broad reach. 'Take it at full tick, shall we Ivor?' I called from the wheel.

'Why not?' he yelled, hanging outside the port shrouds.

'O.K. Take your time. Jump forward when you go – take the pace off it. Land like a cat, old top.' The Instructors in the bow looked aft, wondering if I'd ease the sheets and slow down; others were hoping not.

Perhaps the rubber dinghy came up rather faster than Ivor expected. Maybe we were more heeled than he liked. I was keeping downwind of the mooring to make the jump more difficult.

'*Go!*' shouted the crew. And he went. Leaping raggedly clear of the tumblehome and falling briefly like a leaf. Then he bounced off the side of the inflatable and splashed into the metallic blue water. There was a great cheer.

We shot past the mooring, headed up the loch and came about. Ivor's bedraggled figure was aboard the dinghy, untying from the mooring. When he was clear, I rounded up and picked up the buoy.

Ivor waved his fist but managed a sheepish grin. 'Never mind my cap, I've lost my glasses,' he shouted.

A boat was on its way out from the shore to pick us up. 'I can see the cap, about a hundred yards downwind,' an Instructor said softly by my shoulder. 'It's upside down, floating like a boat; we'll pick it up easy.'

We all clambered down the ladder and into the wooden boat. A couple of minutes later we were round the cap and coming back into the wind. Sympathetic hands reached out as it drew near. A shy Aberdeen doctor scooped it out, as delicately as changing a dressing.

'Och, that's some trick Ivor – yer specs are in the cap!'

· · · — — — · ·

'*And don't let go!*'

Barbara Cartland

Author and Playwright

EPISODE IN 1940

In 1940 after Dunkirk when both my brothers were killed, I was asked to take my children out to Canada because Sir Winston Churchill had said that not only had he intended to 'fight on the beaches' to defend Great Britain but also, he had told his friends, he intended to move all the women and children who were in the South, up to the North of England.

My husband and I thought it over a great deal and we felt that as my youngest son was only five months old it was risking his life to stay because small babies were killed by the blast, not by actually being hit by a bomb.

We went to Canada and I left particulars of where I was with my elder brother's constituents – he had been the Member of Parliament for the King's Norton division of Birmingham – so that they could get in touch with me when they arrived.

The *City of Benares* was sunk and the Government Evacuation Scheme of women and children ceased.

I then knew that I could not take privilege for my children in wartime and that I must return home. I found, however, that I had signed a form saying that I would not return for six months. But that did not deter me!

By getting in touch with one of the most influential men in Montreal I received an extraordinary and special permit to be the only woman with children travelling back on the last ship out of Montreal which carried the Empire Air Training Crew who had been training in Canada.

We found when we got on board that it was the *Duchess of Richmond*'s last trip across the Atlantic because she was going to be a troop carrier.

The Crew had, however, seen the *Jervis Bay* sunk on the way out as the *Graf Spey* was at large in the Atlantic.

We were armed. There were two guns aboard, a machine gun and an ancient anti-aircraft gun. They were manned by day and night ready for any emergency. It was only when the voyage was over that I learnt the disquieting truth that the ship was not built for guns and the submarine gun could only fire sideways, leaving the bow and stern as 'blind spots'.

However, they were a comfort at the time; but I must say that I looked at the very small lifeboat which was ours in an emergency and at the very large icy cold sea, and asked myself if I was crazy to have attempted the journey.

I trailed two lifebelts wherever we went and Nanny carried two as well, and we were always nagging my daughter Raine for forgetting hers.

When we got into the danger zone we slept in our clothes while the small boys' snow-suits were left ready at the foot of the bunks. The ship's doctor told us what to do and explained that we had not only ourselves to consider but the stewards and stewardesses who were responsible for the passengers and had to see that every cabin was empty before they could go to their own lifeboat stations.

'Down perisco . . . damn!'

I cannot say I slept very much. One night I heard a terrific bang and thought: 'Now we are for it.'

I sprang out of bed, picked up Ian's snow-suit, which was lying ready, and suddenly realised that it was very quiet – there were no bells or alarms. I opened my cabin door and looked into the corridor; everything was as usual. I realised that it could only have been a door slamming overhead which had frightened me.

It was then that a feeling of sheer terror took possession of me – we were trapped, we had to go on and forward, whatever happened. Anyone who has been in danger will understand my feelings at that moment – the agony of fear is horrible.

Then suddenly I knew, with an absolute certainty, that someone was with me – not my brother Ronald, but someone I had once loved and who had loved me. He had been killed in a flying accident, but he had been a sailor. He was there as surely as if I could see and hear him. He was beside me, as real and as unchanged in our relationship to each other as he had been when I had last seen him.

I was no longer afraid, my fear had gone, and I knew with an unshakable conviction that he had come to take us into port. I fell asleep, but he was still there in the morning and for the rest of the voyage.

Only when we sighted the coast of England did he go as swiftly as he had come, and I have never been close to him since.

We arrived in Liverpool to find a skeleton of a ship standing out from the river, and smoke rising from many parts of the city as it had been bombed the night before; but there was no sign of the devastation, the panic and the horror which the German broadcasts had tried to convince the world would be found in all parts of Great Britain.

There was a great deal of sorrow and tribulation ahead, but we were home and that was all that mattered.

From *I Seek The Miraculous* by Barbara Cartland (Sheldon Press)

· · — — — · ·

Sir Charles Mackerras, C.B.E.

Conductor

CONDUCT UNBECOMING

Although I have been a keen yachtsman for almost my whole life, having been brought up in Sydney Harbour and now having a boat in the Island of Elba, I have had very few, if any, experiences worthy of inclusion in a book about sailing. On the other hand, I have had a couple of curious aquatic ones, such as the time I conducted Handel's Water Music and Fireworks Music actually on the water, one July evening at St Katharine's Dock on the Thames.

The concert was to be given from the water in a big barge, just like Handel's original performance. We were to be pushed out into the river from the dock and, after playing the Water Music, were to perform the Royal Fireworks Music accompanied by real fireworks. The orchestra, by the way, was the English Chamber Orchestra, augmented for the occasion.

However, on the day of the performance the weather was so inclement, being very overcast but also very windy, that when we put out to sea (or rather, river) the wind was howling so hard *away* from the huge audience assembled around St Katharine's Dock that, although we were playing as loud as we were able, not a note could be heard by them. In fact, the only way of telling when the music was starting or finishing was by *seeing* me wave my arms about while conducting!

Many of the audience complained bitterly and some started to shout at us through loud-hailers; yet others blew their horns in derision from motor launches on the river. Worse was yet to come.

The fireworks had been arranged to mirror exactly the expression of the music – for example, gentle Catherine wheels to accompany the movement called 'La Paix' and whizzing rockets for the one called 'La Réjouissance'. However, as those in charge of the firework display couldn't hear the music either, they got their cues entirely wrong and the whole bang of fireworks came to a huge, noisy climax far too soon, while we were still marooned out in the river waiting desperately for someone to tow us back to land and still frantically and inaudibly ploughing through poor Handel's music over and over again!

Somehow I think that cold summer evening on the Thames served to combine my most embarrassing nautical experience with my most blush-making musical howler at one fell swoop.

. . . — — . . .

'It's all very well for you, mate. I was playing the triangle when she went down!'

'No wind, sea like a mill pond, I'm afraid we're in for a really boring crossing!'

William Sirs, J.P.

Past General Secretary, Iron and Steel Trades Confederation

A NORTH SEA CROSSING

The first time I sailed across the North Sea was as crew on a 30 ft yacht owned by a friend of mine, David Waterstone, who is now Director of the Welsh Development Agency.

After visiting Holland, we were sailing home on a beautiful but windless cold day in the month of May. We had to use the engine and hour after hour we saw the Dutch coast slowly receding in the very clear light of a bright May afternoon.

Because of the lack of wind, we dropped the jib sail and just left it lying on the deck. I was on watch with the skipper until eight bells (midnight) and never have I seen the North Sea in such a placid mood, flat and calm, looking like reflective plate glass. The skipper and I turned in, when relieved, at eight bells. As soon as my head hit the pillow I drifted into dreamland.

The next thing I knew was being rudely awakened by a thunderous crashing sound, accompanied by voices yelling and shouting. My immediate reaction was 'We're sinking!' But on glancing down to the bunk below me, I saw the skipper unaffected by the commotion and sleeping soundly, so I sank back into my bunk and continued my slumber.

Later I found that a Force 7 gale had suddenly sprung up, and this accounted for the thunderous crashing against the bulkhead. And the shouting arose because the jib sail, which we had left unsecured on the deck, had blown into the sea giving our relieving crew the terribly dangerous task of retrieving it.

So the moral of this story is: if you wish to secure sound sleep, first secure your lines. . .

. . . — — — . . .

Katharine Whitehorn

Journalist and Author

AND A GOOD TIME WAS HAD
BY ALL

A party that was entirely agreed about spending the night tied up let their hair down and started a good party going. After two or three hours somebody brightly suggested 'Let's go to sea', so they up-anchored and sailed out hopefully into the liner-infested waters of the Southampton/Cowes area. Drowsiness then understandably overcame them and, reckoning they were still relatively close to land and fairly safe, they threw the anchor overboard and went to sleep.

In the morning, when they woke up, there was no land to be seen in any direction. They were floating freely in the path of the *QE2*, *Canberra*, coastal craft and so forth, the anchor having, inevitably, caught on some piece of chain on its way down since nobody had been sober enough to check that it had actually fallen clear of the boat into the sea.

But, as Bismarck said, 'There is a special providence that protects fools, Americans and drunken men.'

· · · — — — · · ·

'Oh yes, we're quite safe. That 50 lb fisherman's will hold on the first thing it touches!'

Eric Hartwell, C.B.E.

Non-executive Vice Chairman, Trusthouse Forte plc

POURING SEA ON ROUGH OIL

Following a very happy cruise from the river Thames to some of the delightful ports on the Normandy coast, we left Le Havre on board M.Y. *Kandora* on the morning of Saturday, 5 August 1978 at 0045 hours and set course for the Nab Tower. Our destination was the Wight marina which is situated on the river Medina about a mile beyond Cowes on the Isle of Wight. On board was my wife, Dorothy, as well as two friends, Bob and Tessa Holmes.

It was a clear night and, having slept during the afternoon and early evening, I was looking forward to an enjoyable night crossing with the usual interesting experience of passing through the busy main channel, avoiding the ever-circling fishing boats, observing the lights of passing ships with the occasional splendour of a passenger liner and then experiencing the first light of dawn over the horizon as day gradually breaks and the navigation lights give way to actual ships and visual markers.

The ladies had retired and Bob also went to bed. I was kept busy with the constant checking of calculations, radar, depths, course and instruments as well as regular checks on the engine room.

Bob was up and about as we approached the Nab Tower. I had been checking the engine room every hour on the hour and now Bob took over that job, reporting that all was well. Oil pressures, engine and gearbox temperatures were normal, bilge clear and batteries charging – an uneventful and normal trip. As we turned into the Solent, I radioed a message to H.M. Customs and Excise giving our E.T.A. and also to my brother, who lives on the island, since he and some of my wife's family were meeting us at the marina.

Our E.T.A. was 1200 hours and at approximately 1100 hours Bob opened the engine room door for the usual inspection only to find it full of smoke. A rapid survey confirmed that there was no fire but, on further inspection, it appeared that a high pressure hose carrying very hot hydraulic fluid controlling the stabilisers had burst and the result was a mess of smoking fluid all over the forward part of the engine room.

We turned on the reserve extractor fan and gradually it started to clear. A little later Bob checked again and it had cleared enough for him to see the far end of the engine room with the result that he rushed up to tell me that the smoke was clearing but, as he put it, there was a 'waterfall' at the forward end.

It was difficult to see exactly what was happening through the haze but it was obvious that water was pouring in through the top of a plastic lidded water filter, the lid of which was held in position by a butterfly nut. We tried to tighten the nut but to no avail and it was not possible to do much else while the engines were running. In any case, by this time we were approaching the mouth of the Medina at Cowes and I decided to make as fast time as possible to our destination and deal with the problem there. If necessary, I would beach the boat if we were in danger of sinking.

At the marina, the whole family were waiting and two customs officers were there as well as the harbour master. Because it was high tide and we were expected, luck was with us. The harbour master had opened both lock gates as a special welcome, and I took the boat straight through with hardly a wave of acknowledgement and tied up at the first opportunity.

By this time the water was over the walkway in the engine room but, now that the engines were stopped, it was safe to try and get to grips with the problem.

I ignored our welcoming relatives and the puzzled customs officers who were coming aboard, and rapidly stripped to my underpants. Then, to their astonishment and with the floorboards up, I squatted in the oily water only to find that the plastic lid of the filter had buckled and melted with the hot fluid spraying on it. I therefore had to lie down and reach into the water-filled bilge, feeling around until, with relief, I located the sea-cock and closed it, stopping the flow of water.

Our family was slightly bemused at the sight of me dripping with wet oily water and obviously thought me a little eccentric for doing such a thing for pleasure. The customs officers sat there as though nothing had happened, but I had the uneasy feeling that they were slightly suspicious of this diversion from their normal routine.

We borrowed an auxiliary pump and, with that and our own pump, we got rid of the water. The next day we bought all the tins of 'gunk' we could find in the chandler's at Cowes and then spent the rest of the day cleaning, degreasing, scrubbing, flushing and pumping out until the engine room looked like new. I now have a very solid steel water filter fitted below the waterline – which is what should have been there in the first place.

The problem occurred when we were quite close to our destination and when two of us were awake. But the whole trip had taken twelve hours and for many of those hours I was alone at the wheel in the middle of the English Channel making hourly engine room inspections. If the pipe had burst just after one of my inspections the water would have been coming in for an hour, and I might well have been making my first Mayday call – it certainly makes you think!

And, if you're looking to draw a conclusion from this tale, that really is the keyword: *think* before you sink when you go to sea.

. . . — — — . . .

'I say it's the port engine running rough – what do you say?'

Captain Sir Miles Wingate,

K.C.V.O., F.N.I.

Deputy Master, Trinity House

DISPLACED HUMOUR

It was during the winter of 1942 in the North Atlantic, while sailing in convoy, that the following event took place.

I was serving as Third Officer in a German vessel, which had been captured by the Royal Navy off the coast of South America trying to beat the blockade and return to Germany. She was a fine vessel but unfortunately not fast enough to allow us to sail independently nor yet slow enough to steam really happily in a 10 to 12 knot convoy. So each day the Commodore gave us permission to steam around the convoy at full speed, thus clearing exhausts of all carbon deposits and helping to maintain a dark ship throughout the night.

However one day, because of the reports of submarines in our area, permission for a run at full speed was not granted. The report was quite correct as that night we suffered a heavy attack, losing five ships including those two immediately ahead and astern of us. You can imagine that we were all more than a little jumpy, to put it mildly.

Suddenly, with no warning, our funnel put on a show that would have done credit to the Battersea Park firework display.

I leapt to the engine room telephone and the following conversation ensued:

'Jimmy, there are a lot of sparks coming out of the funnel!'

Accompanied by the noise of exploding depth charges dropped by our escorts, which always sound so much worse in an engine room, came the laconic reply from our Fourth Engineer:

'What the bloody hell do you expect, Miles . . . snowballs?'

. . . — — — . . .

Bill Homewood

U.S. Competitor, The Observer Singlehanded Transatlantic Race 1984

THERE'S ALWAYS TWO WAYS
OF LOOKING AT IT

As on previous occasions, I sailed the boat over to England from America on the way to the start of the 1984 Singlehanded Transatlantic Race. Although the boom had broken and I had lost the life-raft during the trip, we'd made good progress on the whole.

It was late afternoon and we were somewhere between Land's End and the Scillies. I put in a VHF radio link call to Tony Powell, the promotions manager of British Airways, the company which was sponsoring my entry in the race. We talked for about fifteen minutes and Tony told me that, although he couldn't take time off from work to meet me, someone would be in Plymouth to welcome me after the crossing.

As I sailed on, I imagined what sort of welcome party would greet me when I arrived. Would there be a brass band and red carpet? I was sure that a company as large as British Airways would arrange something significant for the occasion.

About half an hour after finishing the call I heard the throaty 'chug . . . chug' of a British Airways helicopter. I was so excited! They had obviously arranged a helicopter to fly out specially to greet me! I felt like a small boy coming home to his mother.

As I waved madly and the helicopter took no notice and passed on to the Scillies, it slowly dawned on me that the aircraft was actually part of the scheduled service between Penzance and the islands – and that they never even knew I was there!

★   ★   ★

The Race was now well under way. To solace me in my exile, I had three bottles of rum on board. The first had gone in three to four days. Usually I just toss the empties overboard but this time I thought it would be fun to put a message inside.

I tore a sheet from the log book and put my name, home address, the date, the boat's name, *British Airways 11*, which race I was in, and the latitude and longitude. Then I wrote: 'If anyone should find this message, mail it to me in the U.S.A. and I'll send them $50.' Then I thought: What if I sink? So I added a postscript: 'P.S. If I'm unavailable, please apply to Lord King at British Airways in London for the money.'

Months later, I had reason to go to London and meet Lord King in the course of my work. I told him the story and he replied eagerly: 'Oh yes, I'd pay.' Then, immediately realising in what circumstances it would be necessary to do so, he added lamely: 'But – oh – I don't think I really want to, you know.'

Keith Shackleton

Artist and Naturalist

OMEGA

Beautifully-varnished mahogany dinghies, when taken off trailers and allowed to drop heavily upon concrete, either go 'thud' or 'crunch' according to how much gravel there is between the concrete and the bottom of the hull. It is a situation so universally accepted that a departure from it will always startle those within earshot. A moist sock dropped upon a carpet would straight away become remarkable if, in place of the nearly soundless contact expected, 'boing' were to be heard. It was a fair example, therefore, of the arresting effects of the unexpected when *Omega* was off-loaded from her trailer at Finchinghampton on the first day of Sea Week. When dropped unintentionally hard on the quayside, she went 'clang'!

It must be remembered that this was a long time ago when hulls were made of wholesome wood and plates were of bronze, though a few of the cutters and thrusters had just discovered wood painted to look like metal. Sails were still of Egyptian cotton though the new-fangled nylon spinnaker in *eau de Nil* or 'aice blue' was beginning to be seen. Even yoghurt was still painstakingly cultured from the original bacteria present in the saddle-sores of selected Kurdistan yaks. Looking back on it, we were perhaps at the very end of the era of the genuine – the era of wood, cotton, iron, granite and wool-next-the-skin.

'Clang!' went *Omega* and heads popped up all round. People paused in the shipping of jib sheets, the polishing of bottoms, the scrutiny of shore-hoisted sails. They all stared at the new arrival. One by one they put aside their chores and walked over, and the trickle became a rush. We formed a rubber-necking ring around the strange new boat under its canvas shroud, now being unlaced by her owner/designer/constructor with a nonchalance only possible of the Hon. Clive Leek-Asphodel.

We had all heard something of this boat and all knew the Hon. Clive who lurked at Farnborough in some obscure and finely-screened aeronautical niche. Phugoid oscillations, boundary layer separations, laminar flows and drag were his stock-in-trade and his pocket book fairly bulged with formulae. Moreover he looked the part, squinting myopically at the world through glasses like the bottoms of bottles. The world in its turn looked back at Clive with its usual division of opinion, for while half of it placed him among the greatest scientific brains of today the other half, without lacking affection, regarded him simply as nuts.

Omega was his brain child. She was the last, the ultimate, the *dernier cri*, the boat that would out-class the class and make a nonsense out of Uffa. *Omega* contained, it was said, every last gadget and benefit that the cornucopia of science could pour forth. She had self-aligning this and automatically-shortening that. She had remote kicking-strap adjusters and a spring-loaded mast gate, standing jumpers and gunwhale cam vibrators to lessen skin friction. You could vary the position of the mast, rudder, centre board, jib fairleads and shrouds because she was infinitely variable and possessed more alternatives than a combination lock.

Then came this most horrifying discovery of all – while she was painted all over with the pattern of grain and knots to look like the finest deal, she clanged upon the concrete and the most easily-duped among us knew in an instant she was of tin.

There are few animals more beastly to one another than children when removing Michael from something they wish were theirs. Because dinghy sailors grow old slowly we were all being beastly to Clive. We had just read Nevil Shute's *No Highway* and therefore knew all about fatigue and asked Clive if he had calculated how many windward legs *Omega* would take before she fell to bits. If anybody was charitable to Clive it was Haemish Brambles, who in many ways spoke the same language, and they soon got their heads together in the way engineers and boffins do.

Ignoring the irrelevant and facetious comments of the rabble they went straight to the technicalities. Together they craned into the bowels of the boat where Clive pointed out his epicyclic idling sprockets, his tapered thrust shafts, his reversible gudgeons, his grometless toggles, and Haemish was impressed. Not so much, he admitted later, by the necessity for such apparently heavy mechanisms in so small a boat, but by the sheer academic brilliance of their engineering. Brambles was, after all, a purist. Had his quixotic love of machinery not been well tempered with practicality, he might himself have perfected an invention as brilliantly conceived as it was useless.

One of the features of *Omega*, I recall, were some long shafts with threads on them which ran fore and aft and on these were set some of those robust butterfly nuts one associates with old-fashioned trouser presses. Brambles and Clive were spinning these along, jamming various things in various positions, taking up the slack here and there and drawing the occasional groan of protest from the structure. These were of the slow and purposeful type of mechanical device akin to those cunning forestry winches which hook on a cable so that by idly flexing one's wrist as though ascertaining the time, one may pull a hundred-year-old elm out by the roots. It seems that one must know what one was doing when spinning these racks around or one might do oneself a mischief.

'Check your verniers *before* moving your main aft hoist,' Clive was saying, 'and disengage your thrust pinnion *before* tensioning your athwartships aligning beam . . . O.K., now you can screw down your locking plunger. Now your distances are fixed on your hog and you can read off your differentials on your sliding scale.'

Brambles read off his differentials and was enraptured.

At this point *Omega*'s 'chief engineer' arrived – Giles Purslane. He was wearing white overalls and black shoes and a blue and white polka-dot silk choker, and strapped to his knee was a test pilot's pad and Dalton Computer. Without a word he settled himself on the gunwhale and began taking readings.

Giles was just what one sees in instrument-packed prototypes, dutifully recording the faces of a hundred juddering dials with a note book in one hand and a sick bag in the other. Aviation, out of the rigours of its calling, has certainly sired its own brood.

'Has she been afloat?' I meekly enquired of Giles.

'Only in the tank – this will be her début. The sail plan model has been in the wind tunnel up to force eleven with excellent results.' He licked his pencil and wrote down two six-figure numbers.

Now I would like to tell you a real success story because there is nothing more stimulating than man's triumph over obstacles, but I regret to say *Omega* offered no such opportunity.

Lining the harbour wall like guillemots on the Farne Islands, we watched her wheeled down to the beach for a trial spin. The Hon. Clive, debonair in his white overalls, stepped nimbly aboard and Giles stowed the tool wrap. A few minor mechanical delays with sail hoisting and they were away.

Omega, from our angle, seemed to float low in the water and she appeared to lift the ponderous quarter-wave of a keel boat, but the sun was on her sails and she looked a picture, bobbing gently out between the arms of the harbour into the gentle largo of the outside swell.

One or two of the younger enthusiasts followed her in their dinghies and appeared, from our angle, to gain upon her with remarkable ease rather as a breeze-blown swan's feather will overhaul a floating orange. Through binoculars *Omega* now looked a little lower in the water and there was discernible anxiety in the posture of her two occupants. Again a moment or two, and I witnessed a sight I have never seen before or since with a racing dinghy – she sank!

Clive Leek-Asphodel and Giles Purslane were picked up by a passing ship of the same class but of earlier design and when they came ashore they seemed lost, like men walking in a dream. Everybody was commiserating, the crowd shouted a heartfelt 'Hard luck!' and Haemish Brambles looked as though he were bereaved.

'Do you realise,' he said, 'there were well over three million possible combinations of settings for mast, boom, rudder, sails, plate and shrouds, to which Clive's grandchildren could have devoted a lifetime's research – now all is lost, with the only certain knowledge being that the first position was not very good.' He walked dejectedly away along the quay to buy himself a doughnut.

Clive and Giles left in their car and I have never seen them since, yet my memory refuses to erase the sight of *Omega*'s gunwhales, her boom, her sail number and finally her racing flag impassively consumed by the deep. Then, most poignant and evocative of all – oil coming to the surface.

From *Yachts and Yachting*, 23 February 1962

. . . — — — . . .

'And, for really fine tuning, this gives a ten to one purchase on the kicker.'

Leslie Crowther

Actor and Entertainer

CRUISE CONVERSE

If you're no sailor, but happen to like the sea, one of the best ways to enjoy yourself is by taking a holiday cruise on a luxury liner. And certainly one of the best ways to earn money as a cabaret artiste is to be employed on one.

Admittedly, it's hard work and you have to be gregarious by nature since you meet your audience not only during your act but also at breakfast, on deck, in the pool, onshore – in fact, everywhere!

Dickie Henderson and I were once engaged to perform on the *QE2* and had a whale of a time. We were also together when a member of our audience made one of the classic remarks of all time. It even beat the ship's doctor's comment when he described the liner's jacuzzi as a 'subliminal enema'.

Dickie and I were leaning on the ship's rail one evening watching Lisbon recede into the distance. One of the passengers, a bluff Welshman, decided to make our acquaintance by insinuating himself between us and leaning with his back on the rail. By this one skilful movement he immediately engaged our attention at point blank range.

'Bloody marvellous, you both were,' he said. 'You, Dickie – don't mind if I call you Dickie? – sang and danced and cracked jokes for over an hour. An *hour*! Great! And you, Les – don't mind if I call you Les? – also did an hour. Cracked jokes, did the Flanagan and Allen bit, played the piano, mucked about. Great!' Then came the pearl. 'Of course,' he said admiringly, 'I could never do what you do. I've always had to *work* all my life!'

To this day he is probably wondering why Dickie and I spent the next five minutes having hysterics.

. . . — — . . .

Alan Wynne Thomas

British Competitor, The Observer Singlehanded Transatlantic Race 1984

SPIRIT OF COMPETITION

It all started with the Ice Report, issued two days before the start of The Observer Singlehanded Transatlantic Race 1984.

I handed over a copy to a veteran American singlehanded skipper with a bull-horn voice in the quiet of the lounge of the Royal Western Yacht Club. This year there were 1050 of the deadly icebergs instead of the usual 50 strung out silently like a barrier reef on the Grand Banks of Newfoundland waiting menacingly for us.

After one glance he bellowed in full voice, 'Holy Mary, Mother of God, we're all going to die!' Club members choked over their pink gins and most of the O.S.T.A.R. skippers went off to redraw their routes.

That's how, fifteen days and 2200 miles after the start of the race, John Mansell, an experienced New Zealander sailing the smart catamaran *Double Brown* and I came to be on converging courses as we aimed to skirt the ice limit 400 miles off Cape Race, Newfoundland.

It had been a lively couple of weeks with strong head winds dispersing the 93 starters and already taking a toll of what eventually resulted in 29 retirements or sinkings.

Jemima Nicholas and I had pushed along nicely despite having to tack in mid-Atlantic to avoid the looming bows of the French weather ship as it circled ominously changing station. The weather forecast I had requested could, unfortunately, only be provided in French. They did however, inform me that 'all the French yachts passed by two days before'. Very encouraging!

For nearly an hour in the cold grey morning of Sunday 17 June, John Mansell had been working his MF radio without success to try and tell the outside world that the cross-beams of his catamaran were breaking apart. Finally, running out of options, he had tried his local 40 mile radius VHF radio and caught me dozing in my sleeping bag in shorts and sweatshirt.

Our initial exchanges were fairly laid-back but both of us were pleased to have made contact. My short wave ham set, broadcasting now legitimately in an emergency rather than as an unlicensed bootlegger, seemed to have more success than John's MF and soon the Sunday morning hams, deep in their radio sheds back in Europe, were picking up my crackly PAN PAN call. 'DJ4UQ', Gerd in Frankfurt, passed me on to 'G3CDK', Dick in Wallington, who alerted the Royal Western Race Committee and eventually the British and Canadian coastguards.

They knew now what was going on – but I still had to find him. Our VHF conversations showed the effect of fifteen days' solo cumulative fatigue as we tried to work out whether we were five or forty-five miles apart. It turned out to be ten. And instead of it being like threading a needle in mid-Atlantic, the two needles of his catamaran nearly threaded me. There's nothing in the manuals about how a monohull approaches a multihull in a six foot swell and a cold wet 20 knot plus wind – it certainly isn't straight down the middle!

Stainless steel protuberances on *Double Brown*'s twin stems and sterns threatened to pluck at my shrouds and running backstays and he was obliged to scamper from hull to hull as I ground alongside first his starboard, then his port floats.

His accuracy in tossing his equipment into my cockpit as I circled fourteen times could only have come from years of practice in 'throwing the welly boot' competitions back in New Zealand, and soon the only removable items left were himself and the white mushroom-shaped 'Argos' emergency transmitter with which all boats in the race are required to be equipped. On *Jemima*'s last pass John leapt neatly across the gap between the two boats but the 'Argos' plopped into the water and began floating away still bleeping like a hi-tec Portuguese man-o-war jellyfish until we flicked it aboard with the boathook.

I poured John a large Scotch to go with his fried breakfast as he adjusted to my monohull's angle of heel and I apologised for my earlier VHF remark: 'Don't worry, that's what we monohulls are here for in this race . . . to clear up after the multihulls!'

Double Brown faded quickly and sadly into the distance as I turned again for Newport, Rhode Island, and John slept.

· · ·   —   —   —   · · ·

Keith Taylor

Editor, Sail Magazine

ME AND MY GAFF

The breakwater at the mouth of the Connecticut River was just dropping from view as the first hints of trouble surfaced. In other circumstances I might have heeded them but I was buoyed by the euphoria that came from a week of frantic non-stop preparation culminating in a marathon twenty-four hour work session, plus the elation of being at sea again after two years ashore.

Klang II, our fifty-year-old gaff-yawl was headed for the Storm Trysail Club's biannual Block Island Race week, only about fifty miles distant across a relatively benign patch of ocean. It was a milk run, or it should have been.

It had been a steadily accelerating rush to finish paying the decks, to rig the new mainmast and complete all the other refitting details that an aging wooden 46-footer demands but I was still on schedule to arrive for the start of race week. I had to get there. I had a commitment to produce a daily sailing newspaper. True, the bilge pump wasn't installed, nor was the big heavy canvas gaff mainsail bent on. The only anchor and rode was the clumsy 45 lb Admiralty pattern hook with its attendant ⅜ in chain coupled to frozen windlass. And, yes, the black-painted topsides had opened somewhat after two years. They had alternately baked in the summer sun and dried as we heated the boat to livable temperatures in the dry, cold Connecticut winters.

Our crew could have been stronger too. There was me, the skipper, relatively boat-wise but green around the gills when it came to heavy old gaffers. There was Harris, the old Aussie, a great small boat sailor and shipmate but beginning to show his age. There was my wife, and my employer's wife and her two children aged eight and eleven respectively.

More than one wise man has noted that calamities spring from a chain of small compounding incidents. I was cheerfully stringing together a memorable chain of errors, but I was blind.

We had carried the last of the tide down the river from Essex but now it turned against us. Our little Volvo 15-horse diesel was no match for the combination of easterly headwind and adverse current so we motored, stationary, a mile or two short of Plum Gut, the opening at the top end of Long Island Sound that would spill us into the open Atlantic. We needed horsepower. I was ready to bend on the big mainsail but Harris, older, wiser and fresher, cautioned against it. He was right. We were short-handed and now the boat was pitching and rolling. Lacing the heavy canvas to the gaff, the mast hoops and the seemingly endless mainboom would be a big job.

Clearly this would not be a 5 knot average speed cruise. Instead of the ten or twelve hours we expected to take, it would be more like eighteen or twenty. We finally cleared the Gut after six hours of stemming the tide and as dusk approached we pitched, rolled and putt-putted our way to Block Island. By now the extent to which *Klang*'s wonderful old pitch pine planks had dried out

was fully apparent. On every roll gouts of water spurted through every seam. There was no electric pump so we pumped twenty minutes in every hour, telling ourselves with every stroke that soon she'd start to tighten up. It was a long night.

The dark hours before dawn found us in dense fog and a flattening sea, feeling our way into Block Island's Great South Pond. There was one close brush with an uninviting stony beach but the second time we got it right, sliding gently down the narrow channel into the Pond.

At dawn, with burning eyes and sodden brains, Harris and I surveyed the pristine flanks of the assembled ocean racing fleet as we coasted to our chosen anchoring spot. Harris took the wheel as I began to manhandle the unwieldy anchor over the side.

It was then that the fussy 44 ft coastguard cutter slid across our bows, announcing to us and the entire fleet at about 100 electronically-boosted decibels that we were lost and ordering us to anchor. Exhausted, dazed and dumbfounded, I reacted automatically and began to let the anchor go hand over hand. And about the time that the first 150 pounds of anchor and chain went over the side I knew I had just erred again. I couldn't hold it. I threw everything clear and leapt back as rusty chain roared from the hawse. *Klang* accepted the final insult with equanimity. The whole boat shook as the chain reached the bitter end, but it held. We had arrived.

Explanations made, the coastguard departed. I sat on the foredeck surrounded by well-found, well-crewed smart ocean racers and recalled the corners I'd boxed myself into, the risks I'd taken, the responsibility for others lives I'd accepted so casually. It was a black moment. I even began thinking of a farm ashore.

It was Harris who got me back on an even keel. He sauntered forward, hands in pockets, cocked his head and pronounced in his soft, slow, Aussie drawl: 'She'll be 'right, mate. Weeps enough to keep her sweet.'

. . . ▬ ▬ ▬ . . .

Steve Race

Broadcaster, Musician and Author

GOOD INTENTIONS

As a lecturer on one of S.S. *Uganda*'s educational cruises it was suggested to me that, after a week away from Britain, some of the kids on board might be growing a little homesick. Would I, as a safely avuncular type, mingle discreetly with them on deck and see if anyone looked unduly pensive, even a bit weepy?

Yes, of course I would – especially if it meant a few minutes' chat with one of those attractive teenage girls I had noticed varnishing their nails at my lectures.

Sure enough, there was one – slender and long-haired, leaning over the rail and gazing out to sea. I went over and joined her. We scanned the horizon together in silence.

I put on my most reassuring voice. 'Feeling a bit homesick?' I ventured, slightly sickened at my super-avuncularity.

She turned on me a dazzling smile. 'Atcherly,' she said, 'ah'm dryin' mah hair. But you can talk to me if you want to.'

'Play it again, Salmon!'

Lieutenant-Colonel The Lord Burnham, D.L.

Chairman of the Sail Training Association

TO DEAUVILLE AND BACK

A 60 ft sloop with very basic engine and no reverse gear sweeps into the lock at Deauville, all sails down on a following wind, at the last moment before the lock closes.

Frantic French lock-keeper tries to wave her away.

Skipper in his best French: 'Mais, Monsieur, nous n'avons pas une derrière.' We get in!

* * *

Same yacht returning from Deauville after a very good dinner and a night passage finds herself off the coast of England without any very clear idea of her position.

Lovely summer morning but only 200 or 300 yards visibility.

A small boat seen anchored with fishermen aboard.

Determined to preserve the reputation of their distinguished Yacht Club, the crew lower Blue Ensign and hoist French Ensign.

On approaching fishing boat, Skipper asks: 'Bonjour, Monsieur, où est Littlehampton?'

Fishermen, with unusual linguistic ability, point in the general direction of the shore and shout: 'Par là, Monsieur.'

Same skipper shouts: 'Merci Monsieur,' comes on the wind and disappears into the mist re-hoisting his defaced Blue Ensign as he does so.

· · · — — — · · ·

'Now! Full reverse!'

Jack Higgins

Novelist

IN SEARCH OF EXPERIENCE

It was the summer of 1975, the time at which *The Eagle Has Landed* was published in the U.S.A. I was naturally very anxious to see how the book would be received in America. Would it be a best-seller? I was on tenterhooks. So while all this was happening I thought it would be a good idea to get away and went with my family to Rock, a small Cornish village on the Camel estuary, which boasted a very good sailing club.

Now, I am not a sailor but I was persuaded by my eldest daughter, Sarah, to go out on the water with her. She was taking sailing instruction with the school who supplied a small fleet of Wayfarer dinghies.

Generally, I had turned down her offers to sail because I was rather preoccupied with work on a sea story which later became famous as *Storm Warning*, a tale of Germans sailing a square rigger during World War II. While researching the book I had spent an enormous amount of time reading up about square riggers and interviewing old men who were Masters in sail. I had a mass of technical information but it was Sarah who hit the nail on the head when she said to me: 'The one thing you're *not* doing for this book is actually sailing. You ought to come out with me – even if it is only in a Wayfarer.'

The wind was rather brisk the day we went, about Force 4 or 5, so the instructor proposed that we should keep within the mouth of the estuary for safety. Having rehearsed the inevitable 'Man Overboard' drill we sailed off, but quickly met with a couple of bad squalls and the instructor decided that we should turn back to shore.

We tacked. As we did so, I was thinking about my book and the sequence when the barquentine is wrecked off the west coast of Scotland on Washington reef. This was to be the climax of the story. Suddenly I thought: 'What is it *really* like to be in the water under such terrible conditions?' And, in a flash, I went backwards over the side of the boat to find out.

It was an act of madness. The waves were breaking so high that I couldn't even see the dinghy which was, by now, a considerable distance away. I was wearing a life-jacket; even so, I was appalled at what I had done and paralysed by panic. I didn't know what to do: I was sure I would drown. And, in that moment, I realised the true meaning of terror.

Suddenly I came up on a crest and the boat was right there, beside me. I was aware of a hand reaching down and a line. I grabbed the line and hung on grimly. More hands reached down and I was hauled back over the side.

The instructor was enormously angry and swore that he would never take me out again.

People have mentioned the incident to me many times since it happened. They talk of the need for authors to get authentic experience and treat the whole thing as a joke; they say I took things a bit far and was lucky to get away with it.

But those fifteen minutes in the water made me able to write the wreck sequence in *Storm Warning* with a powerful inside knowledge without which the scene, however carefully worded, would have remained a description, not a truth.

. . . — — — . . .

'*One minute there he is in front of us, then – bam! He disappears.*'

Giles Chichester

Managing Director, Francis Chichester Ltd

TWO FOR THE RODE . . .

In October 1978 I was in Las Palmas harbour, Gran Canaria, with *Gipsy Moth V* preparing to escort a flotilla of nine Pelle Pettersen Maxi 95s across the Atlantic to Antigua. They had been shipped down from Sweden and were still being fitted out when we arrived. The authorities permitted the boats to be moored alongside the inner harbour wall for working purposes during the day but required them to be moved at night.

One evening there was a breeze pinning the boats to the harbour wall and, not having enough space to spring off, one next to the wall was unable to pull away. Those of us on the wall decided to help by pushing the bows off to give the skipper a chance to motor out without hitting the vessel ahead or scraping the side of the boat.

I found myself close to the bow with a long pole we had conveniently located, giving a good shove. Predictably, it proved easier than expected. The bow swung out smartly and I rapidly found myself forming the arch of a bridge which duly collapsed into the dirty, oily harbour wall.

Fortunately, past experience of falling in prompted me to spread the fingers of my left hand to prevent my watch coming off should the clasp come undone in the water and to grab my spectacles with the other hand.

This naturally caused much amusement to all my friends ashore who might well have left me to fend for myself had I not been able to point out that I had the car keys safely in my pocket and everyone would have some difficulty going anywhere without me!

★ ★ ★

My second story is about someone else's misfortune while sailing across the Indian Ocean in *Gipsy Moth V* in the second leg of the Parmelia Race in 1979. It concerns problems of communication in a multi-national crew combined with the technical difficulties involved in familiarising oneself with the plumbing on any yacht.

On *Gipsy Moth V* we had 'Baby Blake' heads – slightly primitive by today's vacuum-pumped standards, but they performed valiantly throughout a long career aboard the yacht. Effective performance, however, depended upon following the right sequence of turning on and off the two hull-fitted sea-cocks as well as the secondary cock on the seawater pump.

The following is a verbatim quote from an entry by another member of the crew in the log for the morning of 4th November:

'In the early hours of this morning, an unfortunate Polish gentleman, a guest of this establishment, met with a nasty accident while abluting.

Without wishing to dwell upon his misfortune, if the gentleman were to study Pascal's principle and apply it to the practice of sewerage engineering, he might well have avoided showering himself and most of the heads with expletive deleted.'

Our earlier attempts to explain the workings had clearly failed and our man paid the penalty of leaving the sea-cock closed while pumping out furiously and building up pressure in the system. 'Guy Fawkes' day came twenty-four hours early in the southern hemisphere that year!

'*You don't suppose those fenders have popped out again?*'

Leo McKern

Actor

JUST PART OF THE CAST

I have a disconcerting suspicion that I am an involuntary member of a large and un-select club. It has no name but would probably be called 'Lubbers'.

The request to recount a short tale of a humorous but factual nature and with a sailing background rings an only-too-familiar and dreaded bell that tolls dismally through the fog of memory.

The actor easily recalls such a request for it bears similarity to the question always asked by the hopelessly unimaginative interviewer, scraping the bottom of his barrel which never contained much anyway: 'What is the funniest thing that ever happened to you on the stage? . . . or the filmset? . . . or in the television studio?'

Alas, the actor's voyage through his career is beset by the same reefs, shoals and storms that he encounters when he takes to the water in an attempt to gain a respite from them, so that memories of time afloat dredge up more blunders and blushes than triumphs.

But of course, one man's horror is another's delight, so. . .

In Dingle harbour at the pier end, preparing to sail. Foul ground astern and to port. Starboard side snug against the pier end, bow pointed due south. Jib up and free, wind 4 knots from the south-west, and the owner engaged with the local off-duty trawlermen in the perennial debate about whether my sloop would take off due south. I knew that it would but some of the square-rig-minded old hands remained unconvinced that *any* sailor could take off into a wind. The mystery of the Bermuda Triangle prevailed even here.

Rudder centred, cast off for'ard, sheet home the jib.

My sweet craft moved forward not at all. The bow swung smartly to port and puttied the twin keels to the bottom.

As I freed the jib and motored off the sand, I reminded myself to explain to the grinning 'Dinglers' that I *would* have headed south had I remembered to cast off aft.

. . . — — — . . .

John Martin

*South African Competitor, The Observer Singlehanded Transatlantic Race
1984*

SHIPS THAT PASS. . .

During the O.S.T.A.R. 1984 I was having an extremely tense race with my
good mate, Warren Luhrs, whom the tipsters had backed to beat me for line
honours amongst the monohulls.

On day five I had radio contact with land for the first time to find out that I
was lying sixth overall behind the multihulls and was actually ahead of
Warren. This obviously pleased me greatly after having had five days of good
strong windward work.

Unfortunately, on this fine morning the wind had begun to ease and signs of
fog appeared on the horizon. Just at this time I spotted a sail behind me close
to the horizon and my immediate thoughts were that it was a multihull
catching me in the light conditions.

Voortrekker II was not going paticularly well in light airs during that race
and I gave an extra bit of effort, hand-steering and continuously trimming the
sails, all to no avail. However, as this yacht got closer and closer it was
eventually identifiable as a monohull and none other than *Thursday's Child*,
sailed by my friend Warren.

By this stage the visibility was rapidly closing in and a dredger, later
identified as British, was approaching on a course such as to pass between our
two yachts, now approximately three miles apart. I called the ship on the radio
to ensure that she had sighted us prior to the fog setting in completely.

As is normal at sea, the Officer of the Watch had a brief chat saying where
he was from and where bound. I then replied that I was competing in the
O.S.T.A.R. and that the yacht behind was also singlehanded and, in fact, my
competition for line honours in the monohull class – adding that it was quite
unique to be so close in an ocean race at a range of 1200 nautical miles from
the start.

He did not share my enthusiasm, unfortunately, and his only reply was,
'Sounds like a pretty lunatic thing to do. . .' Great encouragement from the
first person to sight you in the middle of an ocean!

Later in the day Warren caught me up and passed at a range of 100 feet. It
was nice, in a way, to speak to somebody face to face. We deliberated on
sharing a cheese and wine luncheon but decided against it as the rules did not
allow that sort of thing!

Thursday's Child was going very nicely in the near millpond conditions and
the skipper was free to walk around the boat, eventually deciding to haul out
his video recorder complete with stalk microphone. As they flopped (he and
his boat) off ahead *en route* to Newport, Rhode Island, Warren shouted to me
to 'say something' as he was recording the event for posterity. This was
altogether too much for me at the time and I shall never repeat the first words
that came to mind. . .

'And I hear you are very confident of beating Tuesday's Baby this time.'

Commodore J.F. Wacher,

C.B.E., R.D.

Master Mariner

MAN OVERBOARD

'I know of no place so lonely as a small boat in a rough sea on a dark night.'
Samuel Pepys, off Tangier.

★　★　★

At two-thirty in the morning, the alarm 'Man Overboard' was sounded. The emigrant ship S.S. *Chitral*, on passage from Fremantle to Aden, was pitching and sliding in very rough south-west monsoon seas in the Gulf of Aden. A half-waning moon mostly hidden by low, dark scudding clouds gave bare light as the liner turned on her track and prepared to lower and send away the sea boat.

Commodore Geoffrey Cornish Forrest, in command, was a superb seaman fortunately for the boat's crew. I was a very young second officer and went away with the fourth officer in the 26 ft clinker-built open motor lifeboat. Our crew was made up by a young engineer officer, surgeon, radio officer and five Indian seamen. We got unhooked and clear of the black hull of the ship easily enough, rode out a little on the boat rope and slipped. Up until then there had been little or no time for thought, only action.

The sea was really wild with hissing breaking wave crests and a swell large enough for us to disappear into and be no longer able to see the *Chitral*. We managed to keep head to sea and swell and make bare headway. We were unable to proceed outside the lee of our ship and realised that it would be unwise to do so; otherwise, our boat was staunch and shipped little water.

We sighted and recovered the lifebuoy but there was no sign whatsoever of anything else. . .

After searching for what seemed like an age we were recalled by Morse lamp. Hooking on was a terrifying experience but we made it eventually. As we reached the boat deck rail, 40 feet above the sea, the Commodore leaned over the Bridge and coolly ordered us to lower away back into the tumbling sea. 'Your forward fall is fouled,' he said simply.

When we eventually got safely back on board we learned that two Somalis had been fighting and gone overboard. . .

I don't think that I have ever been so frightened in my life, before or since.

. . . — — — . . .

'Been here long?'

The Very Rev. A.H. Dammers

Dean of Bristol

TALE FROM THE PULPIT

As a junior officer in the Surrey and Sussex Yeomanry during the Second World War, I enjoyed brief opportunities to go sailing at Muizenberg, near Cape Town, *en route* for Egypt, in Alexandria harbour after the El Alamein campaign and in Taranto harbour after the invasion of Sicily and southern Italy. This latter almost proved disastrous.

The Italian Navy ran a sailing club on the harbour and the staff there were anxious to please their new allies. So, one fine morning, I set out in one of the club dinghies to explore the harbour.

The sky grew overcast and the offshore breeze stiffened. Suddenly, with a sharp crack, the mainsail split from top to bottom. In mounting waves, I began to drift towards the open sea. The jib, however, gave me just enough way to fetch up against the outermost ship in the harbour, an American freighter.

As I bobbed up and down alongside, a stream of effluent from a waste pipe disgorged itself into the dinghy. It seemed an age before someone spotted me but at last a rope ladder was lowered. I secured the dinghy and gratefully climbed on board.

The Captain was kindness itself, offering me clean clothes and a large whisky. He radioed the Royal Navy and an immaculate launch came out to tow me ignominiously home.

. . . — — — . . .

'Friendly little chap – he's still waving.'

Eve Bonham

Auctioneer and Lecturer

ACTION REPLAY

My first 'ocean' race was the 1974 Round Britain and Ireland Race with Clare Francis in her Nicholson 32, which was named *Cherry Blossom*.

As the only all-girl crew in the race, we were subject to considerable teasing from our male counterparts in a friendly sort of way, and also some media interest. Southern Television decided to make a film of the race which was later entitled *Take Two Birds*. They loaded us up with cameras and appropriate clobber and said before we left: 'If anything really interesting happens that you are unable to film immediately, then try to do an action replay.' 'O.K.', we chirruped blithely.

Those who participated in this race will remember that we had some rather evil weather on the second leg – in fact, about one-third of the fleet dropped out of the race during it. Now, a Nicholson 32 is a fairly heavy and strong boat, and we had with us a similarly heavy and 'bullet-proof' spinnaker which we called 'Big Bertha'. (We named all our sails – the light spi was called 'Floating Flossie' and we referred to our ghoster as 'Ghosting Gertie'.)

One gusty afternoon, we were spanking along with Big Bertha aloft, when *it* happened. The fibreglass fitting to which the spinnaker sheet block was fixed aft pulled out of the deck whilst we were doing a modest broach. The sail billowed out and wrapped itself around the forestay and later partially fell into the sea when we were trying to get it down. Chaos reigned for half an hour while Clarrie and I tried to sort out the mess as ropes snaked and thrashed about and the boat lurched continually in a lumpy sea.

At length, we had the sail down and another one up and we were sitting, moderately exhausted, in the cockpit with steaming mugs of tea in our hands and the boat speeding onwards towards the Hebrides on self-steering. Clare slowly turned to me and, grinning, said: 'How about an action replay for Southern TV?' We both collapsed into laughter.

N.B. I'm pleased to say that *Cherry Blossom* came third on handicap in this race.

· · · — — — · · ·

'The hem – *pull it down by the hem!*'

Hammond Innes, C.B.E.

Author

BIG BEN AND THE NUMBER NINE BUS

Though this story was told to me quite a few years back, I feel I must be cautious about names, for it was told to me by a well-known yachtsman about a man who was a household name. The yachtsman, sailing down-Channel with a friend, had put into one of the south coast ports for water and refreshment. That night, as they propped up the bar of a quayside hostelry, the landlord leaned over and said, 'Would you two gentlemen be interesting in making a little money on the side?'

A smuggling job? The yacht's owner, highly suspicious, made non-commital noises.

'Because if you are, then there's another gentleman wot's staying the night here who's mighty anxious to get to the other side. Missed the ferryboat, y'see. He's been going around offering a hundred pounds to anybody who'd take him over. Seems uncommon urgent.'

It was in the days when a hundred pounds was a hundred pounds. The Owner looked at his friend, thoughts of drugs and smuggling and criminals flitting through his mind. 'What's this fellow do for a living, do you know?' he asked the landlord, and the landlord replied that the man was an author. And then he said his name. 'A bit eccentric-like,' the landlord muttered.

So the Owner said he was sailing on the tide next morning and if the Author was on board by 10.00 hours they'd take him.

The Author came on board and, conditions in the Channel being a little choppy stayed in his bunk, which the Owner and his friend thought not unreasonable. In the early hours they picked up the loom of the lights of the French coast and as they closed the port they were headed for the Author surfaced, shaved and dressed in a bright silk dressing gown. With a vaguely wandering eye he enquired where they were. When told, he muttered something about a bus going the wrong way.

Not expecting him, for it was still a little bouncy, they had cleared their own breakfast away. Now they laid the table and asked him what he would like. He said he would like some cornflakes. They served him cornflakes, but he didn't touch them. Was anything the matter? No, but he'd like some bacon and eggs. So they cooked him bacon and eggs and when they served it he shovelled it from the hot plate on to the top of the cornflakes. Then he sat and looked at it, still not eating. They asked if it was to his liking. Yes, he said, but he'd like some marmalade. This he spread over the mixture, then ate the whole lot, declaring it a most excellent breakfast.

Again he asked where they were, and when told he shook his head very determinedly. 'Another Number Nine,' he said, getting to his feet and balancing carefully as he peered up through the hatch. 'Just like the last, going the wrong way.'

'How do you mean, going the wrong way?' the Owner asked, doing his best to humour his passenger. 'We're on the French side of the Channel – and buses don't run around on the sea anyway.'

'Not only going the wrong way,' the Author declared, 'but that's not the right route – the Number Nine doesn't pass Big Ben.'

'Big Ben?' The yachtsmen spoke as one, both of them appalled. They tried to humour him of course, but the Author was adamant.

That was Big Ben, there over the stern, and that was a Number Nine bus close alongside. Then suddenly he smiled. 'Ah,' he said. 'Now I understand – it's you chaps that are going the wrong way.'

You will understand why I have not mentioned any names when I tell you the Author died very shortly afterwards. It was the Owner's friend who carried the Author's bags ashore for him and the great man tipped him a pound when a pound was worth a pound. They split the passage money fifty-fifty as agreed, but nothing would induce the Owner's friend to split that one pound note which he kept as a memento of the strangest crossing of the Channel he ever made.

. . . ——— . . .

'And as for those funny old stories . . .'

Jilly Cooper

Journalist and Author

AT COWES

I detest sailing myself, although I wrote the following piece about Cowes. My only other yachting story is about the one and only time my husband, Leo, went sailing. He got into a rough sea and every time anybody called 'Lee-oh' he said 'Yes?' and leapt up brightly to help – and was knocked sideways by the boom – so he never went sailing again!

★   ★   ★

I am sitting in one of the loveliest gardens in the Isle of Wight, gazing dreamily over the wild buddleia at an innocent blue sea, suffering from acute bottle fatigue, and not giving a damn that nearly all the clothes I brought with me are now drifting away towards Beaulieu in someone else's boat.

Cowes affects one like that – I've been here three days, and am sadly coming to the end of one of the best parties of my life.

It was with some reluctance that I arrived here. Cowes itself looked enchanting – like a peacetime garrison town, with bunting everywhere, the cannons booming, and a fleet of boats in the harbour like a great Armada fretting to be sent to war. On the front you could tell the yachting fraternity from the ordinary trippers because they look so disgustingly healthy, wear faded navy blue, and talk in loud voices.

The races started from the Squadron Club – bastion of the naval establishment. A flotilla of small yachts with soft rose-red sails glided down to the start, a cannon boomed and they were off, surging out into the silver blue, spreading out like a swarm of butterflies.

Cliff Michelmore strode by looking purposeful. 'That's Robin Day,' said a fat woman eating chips.

I had a drink at the Corinthian Club, an august building once owned by Rosa Lewis, who used to lean over and pelt her illustrious patrons with apples as they strolled past to the Squadron with their wives.

Everyone was swapping anecdotes about Uffa Fox (whom the whole island adores) and the way he communicates with his French wife: 'Courage, Yvonne, sol is coming out.' Or, 'Est que le champagne good enough pour le Duc?'

The Duc himself was racing at the beginning of the week, and despite what all the papers said to the contrary, evidently had to retire because he sailed round the wrong buoy.

As the pubs are open all day, one's natural inclination here is to tack from one to another. Cowes with its storytellers, fantasists, friendliness, and lack of urgency reminds one of a healthy Dublin.

On to Dot's pub in the High Street. Dot is a termagant with a heart of gold who's been known, in the past, to tear strips off Max Aitken.

A blimpish sailing type was talking about the Royal Ocean Racing Club: 'Club secretary offered me one of their ties, asked me if I'd like silk or Terylene. Asked him what the difference was. He said "Silk's best for holding up your trousers, recommend Terylene if you want to start an outboard motor." '

By four o'clock the races were finishing. I went down to the front and gazed spellbound as the X boats with their brilliant-coloured spinnakers – striped red and emerald, yellow and sapphire, lilac, orange and black – came floating like children's kites towards us.

A young couple broke off a long embrace to look at them.

'What happens if the wind changes, darling?' said the girl.

'Oh, they do something different,' said the boy, and launched into the attack again.

A sudden tropical deluge of rain sent everyone scuttling into the pubs again. Competitors kept coming in with sopping hair, scarlet faces (talk about red veins in the sunset) and dripping all over everyone.

The wind had changed from North to Nor-West. There was a lot of billow talk. Everyone kept referring to dragons, mermaids and sunbeams, which somehow adds to the sense of enchantment and unreality of the place.

'I've got a twin screw, it sleeps four,' said a man in sawn-off blue combinations. 'Fornicates four, you mean,' said his wife.

A drunk sat down and solemnly wrote a postcard to his dog.

Mornings in Cowes, with the deafening report of the cannons, and the anguished shriek of the ferry siren, are particularly equipped to punish a hangover. In a moment of insanity, the night before, I had accepted an invitation from David Dimbleby to go racing on his X boat. Scared out of my wits, I sat feeling sick in the Ladies of the Island Sailing Club. Judging by the juggernaut ladies in there with their booming voices and yachting caps, it might easily be mistaken for the Gents.

One with bruised, mottled thighs as big as oak trees was clad only in a vast flowered panti-girdle. Mesmerised, I watched the roses and petunias spread on her bottom as she bent over grunting to put on a pair of men's socks.

The crew were going down to the landing stage, carrying cartons of pale ale and wearing gaping oilskin dungarees, which made them look strangely vulnerable, like the third little pig who finally routed the big bad wolf.

On the boat I dressed myself from top to toe in oilskins, while David Dimbleby and John Spicer, his co-owner, leapt about pulling bits of string and muttering incomprehensibly about letting out sheets and repairing horses.

The worst bit was when the boat left the moorings and the sails kicked up an hysterical rattling. Off we went down to the start. An ugly grey sea was roaring around us, the teeth of the waves glinting evilly out from the grey. Swallows and Amazons for ever, I muttered through chattering teeth.

Because we were in an X boat contest, some of the other competitors had excruciating names like X-Ray and X-Pectant. Judging from the language that was flashing back and forth, most of them should have been rechristened X-Pletive. The cannon crashed over our heads, and we sailed off well to the front of the field.

After a paralysing ten minutes clutching every spare piece of string I could find, and desperately dodging the boom, I began to enjoy myself. No one shouted at me. We even giggled a bit. The boat flew along like a lark surging in and out of the hills and hollows of the water. We were lying about sixth, and I was just having fantasies about winning and becoming a female Chichester, when we rounded a mark, and suddenly five boats seemed to converge on us, and we were all crashing into each other like dodgem cars.

'Protest!' screamed the man on our right, going purple in the face.

'Ger off!' I said succinctly.

'We'll have to retire,' said John Spicer.

'We can't,' I wailed. My blood was up.

'The man inside me knows I was in the wrong,' said John.

David and I looked at him, wondering if he'd gone all religious on us, then we realised he was talking about the boat on his inside at the mark, so we all giggled and decided to potter about and watch the other races for the rest of the afternoon. The sun came out obligingly and cast a lemon rinse over the water. My hangover blew away. I suppose sailing is just an expensive form of Alka-Seltzer.

Out of the boat, back into the pubs, I felt ten feet tall now and ready to swap merry yarns with laughing fellow rovers. 'I was racing today,' I kept hearing myself say nonchalantly to anyone who would listen.

Finally I changed for the third time that day for the Royal London ball. As it was a naval occasion, I wore a dress appropriately slashed to the navel. A pretty girl called Marcia who was in our party was also changing, and let me put all my clothes in her canvas bag.

The ball was very grand and absolutely marvellous. A huge pink and gold marquee was hung with empty gilded bird cages, presumably symbolising the confines of the married state – there seemed to be a lot of wife-swapping going on.

The men were stunningly good-looking – tall, burnished like Vikings, with steely blue eyes. It was like dining in a restaurant where you wanted absolutely everything on the menu.

Paddy Hopkirk, who was at the next-door table, was busily detonating one of the loudspeakers so it would not blare music in everyone's ears.

'Back in three hours,' he said, going off to dance with a girl in a backless dress.

The evening wore on. Marcia's boyfriend, who looked like a handsome bloodhound, laid his great head on the table among the sweet peas and the champagne glasses.

'He had to get up awfully early this morning,' said Marcia apologetically.

'I'm cheesed off with the navy,' said a pale girl. 'They promised to provide lots of spare chaps.'

'I adore Mr Heath, I just adore Mr Heath,' said a fat woman who was giving the Charleston her all.

It was only when the band played the last dance that I looked for Marcia and discovered she'd taken her boyfriend and all my clothes back to their boat an hour ago. It was sailing first thing in the morning. Somehow it didn't seem to matter.

I wandered back through the town. The lights from the English coast sparkled like jewels, S.S. *Andromeda* floodlit rose out of the black water like a great wedding cake, the tall masts of the yachts swayed across the stars.

If I'm not good enough to go to heaven when I die, I decided, I'd like to go to Cowes.

From *Jolly Super Too* by Jilly Cooper (Methuen)

'I really feel I've arrived now I've got a penthouse mooring.'

Jim Dale

Actor, Singer and Composer

WISDOM TEETH?

While fishing at Pitsea, I was told of a trip the previous week that almost sank the boat with laughter.

Four men were fishing from various parts of a small sailing boat when one called out, 'I think I have caught one!' – emphasising the word *think*, which caused his complete set of dentures to fly out of his mouth and overboard.

For the rest of the day, laughter drove away every other fish in the vicinity but, on the return trip, the friend in the rear of the boat decided to have one last laugh. He tied his own dentures to the end of his fishing line, lowered them gently into the water, then, hoisting them aloft, he yelled to his friend in the front of the boat, 'Look, Jack, what I've caught.'

Jack raced to the back of the boat, took the dentures off the line, thrust them into his own mouth, immediately took them out again and threw them overboard, saying, 'No, they're not mine. Damn!'

The boat arrived back in Pitsea with two men minus two complete sets of dentures.

. . . ———— . . .

'By the way, one of those buckles is a bit dodgy.'

Tony Lush

U.S. Competitor, The Observer Singlehanded Transatlantic Race 1976

A RICHNESS OF EMBARRASSMENT

Going aground is most embarrassing. Exhibiting said behaviour in front of one's acquaintances is worse form and is likely to encourage reminders of the event for several years to come.

Prior to the 1976 Observer Singlehanded Transatlantic Race, I was indulging in some cruising on the western coast of Scotland. My boat, *One Hand Clapping*, had been home-built in Michigan. She had been outfitted with a Chinese lug rig with the mail-order assistance of Jock McLeod, who worked in close concert with Colonel H.G. 'Blondie' Hasler, originator of The Observer race.

Sailing from the Isle of Man, I decided to make my first anchorage West Loch Tarbert. My chart showed the eight mile loch to be about an inch long so I trusted the information in my pilot book to guide me through to the anchorage near the ferry dock at the head of the loch. These instructions suggested that I stay mid-channel, not getting too close to the buoys *en route*.

Running before the breeze, sail was reduced to keep the speed down, but to no avail. Just short of the dock, I swung wide to allow a turn head-to-wind – and went firmly aground on hard sand. That meant it was time for a re-floating programme.

Tide tables indicated that the tide would rise – eventually. In preparation, an anchor was rowed to the far side of the channel and winched right back to the boat. The anchor was again taken across the channel and carefully placed in the fork of a stout-looking tree about 150 metres away. The tree appeared to have good holding ground!

While I started to take up on the line, a young lad rowed out and pleasantly informed me that the tide there came and went approximately every week or two, depending on the weather of course.

From time to time, the rode's tension had to be released to permit the arrival and departure of ferries from the Kennacraig terminal. The departures weren't too bad but the ferry's wash on the first two arrivals drove me even further aground.

Once sufficient tension was gained to keep the line out of the water between tree and boat, I tried to reduce draft by hoisting the dinghy filled with water by the main halyard. Again, no success. The lad with the dinghy took my second 600 ft warp to his house where his father tried winching me from that angle. We didn't budge an inch.

Suffice it to say that only the kind assistance of the ferry's launch prevented my becoming an extra aid to navigation in West Loch Tarbert.

Yes, I was embarrassed for having got myself into that pickle. I was even more embarrassed at being unable to get myself out of it and to need the assistance of others. But my embarrassment was not to be complete until I got back down to Plymouth for the start of the race.

I was already in Millbay docks when I heard that *Ron Glas* was at the customs quay with her skipper Jock McLeod. He had come to Plymouth via the Caledonian Canal and had visited his old cohort, Colonel Hasler in Western Scotland *en route*.

I went to introduce myself to the man who had helped me design my boat's rig by correspondence. And his first words to me were: 'Tony, I heard you went aground up in Scotland!'

The entire nation must have heard about it! Embarrassment complete.

. . . ▬ ▬ . . .

'Wake up, darling, remember that teensy little island you told me to look out for?'

Lady Wagner, O.B.E., Ph.D.

Former Chairman of Council, Dr Barnardo's

BUMP IN THE NIGHT

We had sailed into Amsterdam, tied up and dined well, talking as darkness fell to fill in the time until the railway swing-bridge – which is raised once at 2 a.m. to let the yachts in and out of the canal system leading to Dordrecht and the south – should open.

At midnight, we sailed across the river to take up our position but somehow, at night, the lights made everything look different and we were uncertain about the precise location of the bridge. Suddenly there was a horrid bump and we were aground. For two hours we struggled, pushing and pulling in the water, heaving and tugging to get the yacht off the mud, all without effect. Then, exhausted, we had the mortification of seeing the bridge open and the yachts come streaming out of the canal barely a hundred yards from where we remained firmly stuck.

After what seemed a remarkably short night, we heard a voice calling, heavy with irony: 'Do you want to be where you are?' It was the Dutch harbour authority. Then, having left our dinghy for the first time ever back in England, there was nothing for it but for an intrepid crew member to swim across in the chill waters and collect the tow rope.

Twenty-four hours late, we slipped under the bridge and joined the silent cavalcade of yachts for the magical journey round the canals of Amsterdam, all memories of the previous day's frustrations banished by the pleasure of sailing through a sleeping city by moonlight.

'We're off!'

Donald Sinden, C.B.E.

Actor

HOLE IN ONE

In *The Cruel Sea* all the stunts were done by Frankie Howerd (no, not *that* one). In one scene a British ship has been sunk by a submarine and the survivors are swimming around in oily water. The captain of *Compass Rose* is faced with a Solomon type of decision: shall he pick up all the survivors or blow up the enemy submarine which he suspects is lying immediately beneath them, thereby preventing it from destroying more ships? He decides to blow up the submarine. He steams straight towards the exhausted swimmers who think he is going to save them. . .

This scene had to be done in a series of cuts, one showing the men in the water, another (shot from the stern of a tug) showing the bows of *Compass Rose* getting nearer and nearer, and finally a third showing the bows ploughing into the doomed men. For this a 'cradle' was slung over the side of the ship, two feet above the water, on which were placed the camera and its operator, Chic Masterson. Through the lens the knife edge of the bows could be seen cutting through the water at full speed. A number of lifelike dummies had been placed in the water and Frankie was seen swimming amongst them, then at the very last second he used his hand to push himself away from the prow of the ship, to be carried off on the bow wave under the camera! I tried to watch this scene from our deck, but had to turn away. What a way to earn a living!

For about a week we actors were aware of a major crisis brewing. Each evening at the hotel the producer and director met with the production manager; voices were raised, hands struck foreheads, carpets were paced. Slowly the news filtered through: Alan Webb had been engaged to play the admiral and in the scene to be filmed the day after tomorrow he was to come alongside in the Admiral's barge. The film company had been negotiating with the Admiralty for the use of a barge, but it had proved impossible to secure one – each admiral had his own and there were no spares. By chance Jackie Broome heard of this impending calamity which, unless solved, could necessitate a script rewrite and possibly costly rescheduling.

'Why didn't you ask me?' he roared and picked up the telephone. 'Get me the Admiral Superintendent.' A pause. 'Captain Jack Broome' – a pause – 'Hello Pinkie, Jackie here; look, could we borrow the barge on Thursday? – Very good of you, thanks.' Weeks of correspondence went out of the window. The old boy network had saved the day.

Jackie excelled himself on another occasion. *Compass Rose* had to return to her home port of Liverpool. One dockyard is very like another so Devonport became Liverpool. We were to steam up the Tamar/Mersey, make a sharp turn to starboard into a closed harbour (for the uninitiated this is a man-made enclosure with a narrow entrance where ships may be parked) and pull up alongside a ship already moored at the quayside (double parking). This other

126

ship – nothing to do with our film – was one of Her Majesty's destroyers.

Jack Hawkins was apparently in command, but in fact Jackie Broome was giving the orders while kneeling down and peering through two peepholes specially bored in the bulkhead. My job was to be in charge of the fo'c'sle party of real sailors who, on my command 'Stand by your wires and fenders', prepared to drop the fenders over the side to prevent one ship scratching the other and to pay out the hawsers which would secure us alongside.

Again three cameras were to film this arrival, one on board our ship, one secreted on the quayside and another on top of a crane to get an 'aerial' view.

Under Jackie's orders *Compass Rose* came up the river at five knots, turned to starboard; my order 'Stand by your wires and fenders' was immediately executed and as a result of Jackie's 'Port 15', 'Slow ahead', 'Steady as you go', 'Full astern both', we came to rest nine inches away from the destroyer exactly on the spot required.

A perfect piece of parking.

We all gathered round Jackie to congratulate him. 'How do you do it?' someone asked.

'Experience,' replied Jackie.

Unfortunately two of the cameras had failed to capture this masterpiece. We had to do it again, so back down the river we went, turned round and waited for 'Action!'.

Now nobody could accuse Jackie of conceit but our adulation had made him rather pleased with himself. This time he took us up the river at nine knots, we turned to starboard, on cue I said 'Stand by your wires and fenders,' but to my astonishment I found the crew were already doing it. I noticed the sea was rushing past us . . . Suddenly the whole ship heaved, as our anchor, protruding from the side of the bows, tore a hole nine feet long and ten inches wide in the side of Her Majesty's destroyer!

And there was Jack Hawkins in full view of the bridge – Jackie kept out of sight . . . From the wheelhouse of the destroyer emerged an officer, who, with perfect RN understatement, surveyed the damage and said:

'Who the flipping hell's driving your boat – Errol Flynn?'

From *A Touch of The Memoirs* by Donald Sinden (Hodder & Stoughton Ltd and Futura)

· · · — — — · · ·

The Rt Hon. Sir Edward du Cann, K.B.E., M.P.

Admiral, House of Commons Yacht Club

MARITIME MOTTOES

The height of international happiness –
    A house in rural England, by the sea
    A Japanese wife
    A Chinese cook
and an American salary.

The height of international unhappiness –
    An American wife
    An English cook
    A Japanese house, inland
and a Chinese salary.

. . . — — . . .

'What a peculiar question George. Of course I would want you to re-marry if I die in a sailing accident!'

General Sir Michael Gow, G.C.B.

Commandant, Royal College of Defence Studies

CHANGING TACK

While sailing a dinghy with my son in a creek in the Isle of Wight, another dinghy came towards us manned by two men and ran aground.

As we passed them, we heard one man say to the other: 'Let's pretend we did it on purpose' – and then he fell overboard!

. . . — — — . . .

Sir Leslie Porter

Chairman, Tesco Stores (Holdings) Ltd

NOM DE PLUME

I called my boat, a delightful 54-footer, *Delamare* because my office, at Tesco House, is in Delamare Road, Cheshunt.

Names of boats ring curious bells sometimes and once, just as I was leaving Nice harbour, a sailor came rushing up the jetty towards us, shouting in French that his name was 'de la Mare' and that he would like to come aboard. So I delayed our departure and waited for him to board. But he was so excited on seeing a boat bearing his own name that he ran right into the sea!

. . . —— —— . . .

'*I name this ship . . .*'

Mac Smith

U.S. Competitor, The Observer Singlehanded Transatlantic Race 1984

NOTHING TO QUAIL AT

At the time, there was no humour in the incident although, in retrospect, it brings some smiles. It was, in fact, a moment of panic followed by some moments more of hectic activity to keep *Quailo* off the rocks surrounding the tiny harbour of Santa Cruz on the island of Flores in the Azores.

Sonja and I had departed New Smyrna Beach, Florida in early April. A little too early, for the spring weather in '84 was blustery. I was *en route* to Plymouth to participate in the O.S.T.A.R. and looked forward to the west-east crossing with holidays in Bermuda, the Azores and Plymouth with almost as much anticipation as the race itself.

Our voyage started off badly. Ten minutes away from the marina, *Quailo*'s transmission failed. It literally self-destructed as a bearing came apart and dropped bits of steel into the gears. Sails were hoisted and the winds favoured us that day as we sailed the few miles of inter-coastal waterway to Ponce de Leon Inlet and open Atlantic waters.

A gale set us back in our approach to Bermuda. But, we had no problem sailing through the cut into St George's harbour, nor sailing out again five days later. Though, in the meantime, our newly acquired inflatable – purchased to retire our tired but trusty old Avon – ruptured a seam along its port hull, thereafter being useful only as undesired ballast.

The crossing to the Azores continued to be blustery except for the day of the storm. That day was something more than blustery and, actually, quite spectacular. Sonja took it very well. Particularly in that this was her first ocean voyage.

The winds reached 60 knots. I hauled the last of our mainsail down and lashed it to the boom. Our headsail had been doused sometime earlier and we continued under bare poles for twenty-six hours. At the peak of the storm *Quailo* was running at 12 knots (without sails) and the wind speed indicator pegged at 65 knots.

The following morning our boat speed slowed to 3 knots. I raised a triple reefed mainsail. We had sailed 142 miles without a sail.

But the real adventure, certainly the most memorable part of our voyage, began as we came close under the southern tip of Flores. It was May 1st. We enjoyed a rare bit of sunshine and fair sailing that dwindled to calms with the evening.

We monitor our VHF radio, channel 16, even in mid ocean. Nevertheless, I was surprised when, well past midnight, a heavily accented English voice began calling: 'Sailboat, Sailboat. Are you in trouble?'

Assuming myself to be the 'sailboat', I replied with our radio: 'No, we are not in trouble except that we have neither wind nor auxiliary power.'

Since sundown we had drifted in the lee of the island, only occasionally

'I know I can't fix the engine, but I am sure I could steer O.K. if you would just let me try!'

catching a puff in our sails to drive us along a few yards. The lights on the island had gone out hours earlier when the generating plant shut down. Only the beacon at Ponta das Lajes, with auxiliary power, continued its assigned arc across the waters.

Familia Augusto, the only fishing boat on the island with a deckhouse, was alongside heaving a tow line. Secured, the line came taut and we roared into the darkness, slowing a few miles up the coast as I sensed our approach into a broad cove.

The VHF again. 'You say when water is 8 metres.'

'O.K.' They had no instruments. *Quailo* was navigator.

I called back 10 metres. Then, nervously, 8 metres. The dark cliffs were close.

'You stop now. You stop now.'

I had no way of stopping but circled broadly away from the cliff and let our C.Q.R. anchor slide over the bow roller. It caught the bottom and we swung easily.

Familia Augusto went back to work with a promise to return the next afternoon and tow us to Santa Cruz. Sonja and I relaxed in the quiet darkness, listened to a nearby waterfall dropping to the sea and counted our blessings.

It was early morning, not afternoon when *Familia Augusto* returned. Jose Augusto had aboard not only his crew of sons, but his grandchildren. It was an adventure for them as well.

Two of the boys came aboard to help with the anchor and to pilot *Quailo* to her mooring. We entered the rocky passage to the tiny harbour and picked up moorings just inside a rough volcanic shelf that sheltered the harbour. Too close to the rocks, I thought. But it was the only protected water that would accommodate our eight foot draft.

Five days later, prepared to depart Flores, we relied again on assistance from the Augusto family. Until we reached open water, sailing was out of the question. Bow and stern moorings had kept *Quailo* off the volcanic wall and lines to those rocks protected her from shallow water to port. In exiting, we had to pivot *Quailo* 180 degrees, bringing her bow from north to south; then round a large rock at the end of the breakwater and, clearing that, proceed eastward between the rocks in the narrow approach to open water.

Manipulating lines, we achieved the pivot. Umberto Augusto took us in tow with a small open fishing boat and we cleared the rock at the end of the breakwater. This manoeuvre left our bow heading with the tow boat to the southwest.

Umberto dropped the tow line – I assumed, to allow himself an opportunity to bring his boat about for the easterly run through the approach channel. The winds were northerly at 15 knots but our sails were secured. We could not afford the problems they might create in the close manoeuvring.

'Now go', Umberto shouted.

I was dumbfounded. With the breeze almost dead astern, rocks and shoal water everywhere, it would have taken too long to raise even the mainsail, come to port 120 degrees and sail the narrow channel.

Impossible!

We would founder.

I like adventure and excitement. I passionately dislike the kind of excitement that comes with uncontrolled or unco-ordinated activities aboard my boat.

But I had it! Lots of it!

I shouted, cursed, jumped, waved my arms – all things I despise in sailors. I was despicable.

Umberto got the message. He brought his stern to my port bow, again caught the tow and brought us through the channel.

For the first time, we looked back at Santa Cruz. It appeared that every child, official and townsperson had come to watch our departure. We waved, hoisted our sails and made for England.

· · · — — — · · ·

Erin Pizzey

Founder of First Shelter for Battered Wives and Their Children

MUD LARKS

The only sailing incident that I can remember being embarrassingly involved with was sailing with a girlfriend of mine and two men, John and Robert.

We were on Robert's lovely boat which was very small with a beautiful teak interior. We were sailing down to Chichester. I remember we got stuck in the mud flats and I was used as ballast. I had to sit on the ship's lavatory while they heaved and strained to get the boat off. We finally did arrive at Chichester harbour, smelly, dirty and very tired. And we then had to have dinner at the Yacht Club with everyone else smartly attired and glaring at us over their gins and tonics. So my memory of Chichester Yacht Club is somewhat jaundiced!

Other than that, I love the sea and am one of the few dedicated cooks under sail that I know of!

· · · — — · · ·

'There!'

Warren R. Luhrs

Yachtsman

RECORD JUMP

It was a lovely clear September day, 150 miles off the Georgia coast in the middle of the Gulf Stream. Winds were 12 to 15 knots from the NNW and my boat, *Tuesday's Child*, was moving well with assistance from the Gulf Stream.

We were seven days out from St Petersburg and we expected to clear Hattarass by a wide berth in another day before heading into the Chesapeake Bay for the Annapolis Boat Show.

My crew member, Dave Cook, had just finished lunch and had settled down for a few winks. I was resting comfortably in the cockpit reading a book when I heard a distant 'wop' sound from above; a quick look revealed nothing.

A closer examination showed a dark spot on the main sail, about 20 feet above the deck. It was a grasshopper, about four inches long! Where had he come from? We had been at sea for about a week and were presently 150 miles offshore. He or she (I could not discern) had either hitch-hiked a ride as a stowaway for the last seven days or had just completed the longest, most phenomenal jump ever made in history! I hope the force stayed with him (or her).

'Swat it, Warren, swat it!'

Air Marshal Sir John Whitley,

K.B.E.

Past Controller of R.A.F. Benevolent Fund

SAILING INTO L'ABERWRACH

In the summer of 1969 I set out in my Great Dane 28 with Yvonne Van de Byl and Chris Russell, my stepson, to sail to the Morbihan. We had a pleasant sail from Lymington to Dartmouth and the next evening set out from Dartmouth for L'Aberwrach, aiming to reach there in daylight.

We had, as it turned out, a miserable trip as we ran into dense fog halfway across the Channel. Anyway, we continued and eventually heard the Ile Verge lighthouse booming away. One hour later, as it was getting light, we saw a lobster pot buoy and decided to cling to it and have breakfast until we'd sorted ourselves and our position out.

Halfway through breakfast Yvonne suddenly yelled 'Rocks!' and sure enough we seemed to be in the middle of them. We cast off quickly and motored out on a reciprocal course.

Some minutes later, a French fishing boat appeared out of the fog and I shouted, 'Ou est L'Aberwrach?' to which he answered, 'Suivi-moi, monsieur.' But there was no hope of 'suivi-ing' him as he was going much too fast for us!

The fog lifted shortly after this and we sailed into L'Aberwrach via the Malouine passage.

'Then, just before the giant lobster attacked, the boat was engulfed by an eerie mist . . .'

Peter Cadbury, M.A., F.R.Ae.S.

Company Chairman

THAT'S MY LOOK-OUT

Colinette III was a superbly equipped twin motor cruiser, 70 ft long, fitted with stabilisers, radar, auto-pilot and every gadget available to an enthusiast.

At the time, I was Chairman of Westward Television and I was interested in the return of Francis Chichester to Plymouth. I had arranged to pick up a camera crew and sail out into the Atlantic to take pictures for our news and magazine programmes. The *Sunday Times* heard of this and asked if I would take their camera-man and a reporter. I agreed and arranged to pick them up at Poole harbour.

We set off into very rough seas and it was not long before the camera-man and the reporter were out on deck wrapped in blankets in the lee of the wheelhouse. Some eight hours later we were approaching Plymouth and I radioed ahead for an ambulance to meet us and take off the two bodies, dead or alive.

The Westward team came on board and, after two hours, one wanted to get off so we went into Falmouth to drop him. The rest of us, plus a very attractive blonde girl who just seemed to be doing nothing on the quay at Falmouth, set off into the Atlantic where we met up with Chichester, recorded a conversation with him from his boat to *Colinette III* and took a lot of film. Everyone was happy with what we had achieved: a scoop! We set off to Plymouth to deliver the film and, after a few hours, we sighted land, having first of all seen the outline of the coast on the radar screen.

I identified it as Dodman Point but Geoff Elkins, who had come along as crew and was a professional seaman, argued that it was Nare Head. It was important to know where we were so, as we couldn't agree, we cruised in near the shore where we found a lone fisherman in a small dinghy.

With radio antennae flying in the wind, the radar scanner turning on the mast and all signs of the sophistication of our equipment quite visible, it was shameful having to ask where we were from such a humble mariner in a dinghy. But at least he knew where we were and told us – along with various choice comments about the ignorant owners of smart motor cruisers.

By now we were short of time so we failed to take the blonde back to Falmouth and she ended up in Berkshire!

Shortly after this trip we were going across to Alderney. It was a hot sunny day and, as there seemed to be no other vessels in the English Channel, we all stretched out on the foredeck and set the auto-pilot to steer us to the Channel Islands.

For several hours we lay in the sun until suddenly we heard a shout. I looked up to see a small catamaran obviously becalmed in the oily flat sea. He said he had run out of fuel so we hoisted down a four gallon can of petrol, which meant that he was once again mobile, at least for a time.

It was a surprise to learn, when we got back to Poole, that this man whom we had rescued from a watery grave had reported us for not keeping a proper look-out. Ingratitude knows no bounds!

. . . — — — . . .

'Having cross-checked my Sat-Nav position against my radar-assisted dead reckoning and, bearing in mind that we've just crossed the six fathom line, I can state with absolute confidence that is definitely Dodman Point – or Nare Head, I think.'

Desmond Wilcox

Television Producer

MY BLUE HEAVEN

As a boy of fifteen I did more than yearn for a life at sea – I actually ran away and trained for it and, via the Outward Bound Sea School in Aberdovey and a sail training apprenticeship on a square rigger, I discovered that the spirit of Joseph Conrad and Joshua Slocum had been burning in me since birth.

So it was a series of accidents and mistakes, that took me from the merchant navy into the army, Fleet Street and television. But I stayed true to my first professional calling. At every step I said to Commanding Officers, Fleet Street editors, television directors, and radio producers: 'You know, actually, I am a sailor.'

As a result, for years I have been – naturally – deferred to at parties and B.B.C meetings (almost the same thing) when sailing is being discussed. Mine is not a reputation earned at the gentle summer game of yachting in the Solent, but through experience of the real and salty thing.

Of course, it is thirty years since I was actually employed as a sailor but I do keep in touch. Our bathroom groans with yachting magazines, books on navigation and ship maintenance.

Now, it is true that 'sailing is the thing'. So the fact that my family had agreed to hire a 40 ft elderly diesel cruiser called *Cygnet XIV* on the Norfolk Broads one summer was something of a dent to my pride, salved a little by general agreement that we would tow a sailing dinghy behind. The demonstration by the man from the boatyard on how to run the boat, I treated with personal scorn but as an opportunity for the children to be amused while I busied myself trying to repair, with my new multi-purpose penknife, a cabin door that had come off in my hands because I had tried to open it on the hinge side. Perhaps I should have listened but I maintain that even if I had my eagle eye, trained to spot small details and gaze over distant horizons, could never have spotted that the throttle lever on the boat was, clearly, about to undergo metal fatigue.

It did so half an hour after we left the boatyard, at a time when all the groceries, most of the bedding and vast piles of crockery and china were assembled on the cabin floor and had become the subject of a huge family row, based on the children's wails that they needed their bunks for sleeping and could not surrender them to the storage of provisions and kitchen ware. The lever snapped off just as I was about to make a destroyer captain's approach to the berth in a narrow canal which I had selected as a pleasant place to spend the evening.

Unstoppable and flat out at 6 knots, the elderly *Cygnet XIV* roared straight at an immaculate waterside lawn sprinkled with daffodils, where a family party were seated on their terrace at tea. I nearly reached them too, but brought up short with the last four feet of the hull still in the water. I admit it didn't do the lawn, or the daffodils, much good and I feared that the retired Brigadier whose garden we had invaded would have a stroke. But his wife was most admiring and told me later, in confidence, that her husband had not stammered quite like that since he was a teenager. In the end the Brigadier understood that it was all just as embarrassing for me, a true sailor bred to the old ways of boat handling, and a shocking reflection on hired boats on the Norfolk Broads.

Later that night I had almost imbued my crew with the spirit of true maritime adventure when the cruiser's lavatory exploded. Actually, it is not an uncommon occurrence and one well within the capacity to endure of a strong stomached sailor. It was just a pity that the family debate about where to put the food had resulted in that particular place being used as storage for the cornflakes and bread.

The next day I agreed – and only another 'blue water' man will know what it cost me to do so – to allow the hanging out of washing on a line that I, myself, would rig from stem to stern.

I believe that the moment at which I stepped backwards off the cruiser into four feet of muddy water, clutching the washing line, has become an event to be remembered by my family as dearly as I would like to forget it. I also believe, but I am far too generous to try to prove it, that it was not accidental that my eldest daughter, Cassie, kept saying 'take it a little further back'.

I think it is also useful to note that when the water is only four feet deep – but he doesn't know it – an old salt will still naturally struggle to survive by attempting immediately to get rid of all his heavy clothing, including wellington boots. I only stopped doing this when I observed my young son, Adam, standing waist-deep in front of me, rescuing, one at a time, the perfectly good items of clothing I was hurling further out into the Broads.

A previous editor of *That's Life*, Peter Chafer, was a calm, blue-eyed, pipe-smoking man. He actually owns a 'proper' boat, a cutter made of wood and propelled by wind – largely because the engine is usually broken down – kept in a yard full of small and professional sailing craft on the south coast. Like so many landlubbers, he manages to look even more nautical than those of us who, despite flowered ties and Italian suits, do actually have 'blue-water' experience.

I was not, therefore, surprised when he asked me if I would like to spend a weekend crewing for him with a couple of other friends. One of them was a lady who suffers from an allergy to the sun and therefore arrived wearing well-cut slacks, high heels, cotton gloves, a headscarf and pearls. The other lady confessed that she is sea-sick on Waterloo Bridge. But I loved her, so I didn't believe her.

We had a lovely day's sailing and, by the time we came into the harbour, my wife-to-be, impressed with my nautical tidiness, my expertise, and a few anecdotes she hadn't heard before, was sitting, relaxed, on the cabin top. It was then that I observed, despite Peter Chafer's skill at the helm, we might when taking up our berth brush the side of an already moored yacht.

'Fend it off with your foot,' I commanded the lady. She has, it seems, a capacity to go deaf on occasions which, in years together since, I have observed to be most irritating.

There was nothing for it but action. Holding the bow mooring rope, I leaped for the floating pontoon. They tip if you land on them heavily, from a distance and a height. Not many people know that. I think my two cracked ribs were actually suffered before I hit the water, when I scraped the side of *Sandling*. I went down at once, but surfaced. My friend Peter and the others on the boat were very impressed at the 'Excalibur' way in which I held the rope above my head for one of them to recover, before going down the second time. Peter didn't smile or laugh. He told me that he bit through the stem of his pipe, not smiling or laughing. . .

The 38 ft ketch I chartered for a week's summer cruising in the English Channel, the following year, was moored at Dartmouth. I had been modest when filling in the form, sent by the owners to prospective charterers. Under the section headed 'Previous Experience' I wrote 'sail training school, sail training apprentice on square rigger, various crewing and hiring experience'. A truly British understatement of my nautical worth, I thought.

I took, with my family, a B.B.C. secretary I knew – a strong, smiling girl, the kind that is always described as 'good in emergencies'. She assured me that she had a great deal of previous sailing experience and I felt comforted by this. She didn't mention that her previous sailing had been confined to a dinghy on some kind of pond just off the North Circular Road, nor did she say that she was violently car-sick and sea-sick. She demonstrated one on the way down, and gloomily forecast the other as we climbed aboard *Christmas Rose*. For the initiated, *Christmas Rose* is a Nicholson 38, equipped with every modern convenience, a motor/sailer with, as they say, the emphasis on sailing.

We took her out the next day, raised the sails – and went round the corner half a mile to the nearest bay and dropped anchor, because the children wanted to swim. I grumbled about the shortness of the voyage but decided to humour them.

It was only when the engine of *Christmas Rose* blew up later that evening that I realised quite how much oil there is in a marine engine. Most of it was splattered over the cockpit but a considerable quantity had managed to find its way on to the white yachting jeans of my youngest daughter Claire and the cheesecloth blouse of the sailing secretary Doris. The owner of *Christmas Rose*, when we returned to Dartmouth in the dark and under sail only, admired the way I managed to get back without motor power and was contrite about the engine. He started to mention metal fatigue – and, clearly, didn't understand why I groaned and asked him not to continue.

In Salcombe harbour the next day, the children wanted to celebrate their mother's birthday. We went ashore to do so and returned bearing champagne and turkey sandwiches for supper so that she wouldn't have to cook on her very own day. (In any case, the calor gas had run out and her eyebrows hadn't fully recovered from her attempt to light the emergency Primus stove.)

Now, *Christmas Rose* was equipped with an inflatable tender (rubber dinghy, for landlubbers) and the children's mother was concerned that the turkey sandwiches should transfer from the dinghy into *Christmas Rose* without getting wet. Exactly how the dinghy managed to drift away from under her legs, leaving her suspended by her fingers from the stern of *Christmas Rose*, has been a matter of considerable debate in the years since. But at the time, the excitement was quite intense, particularly when the children remembered that their mother couldn't swim.

She, clearly, hadn't forgotten. One could see her knuckles whiten as she slid lower in the water. Naturally, I attempted to re-start the engine and get back to her, as we were swept out by the tide – away from *Christmas Rose*. Seafaring secretarial Doris thoughtfully threw an oar to her. This hit her on the head and also deprived us of any means of rowing back to her. Eventually a neighbouring yachtsman puttered down in his dinghy and helped her aboard.

Twenty minutes later we rejoined her. The children were tearful but a little amused. Doris was still explaining about the oar. The victim was not speaking to anybody.

Sailing, for me, since then has been little more than a half day here and a weekend there, during which I have observed a continuing deterioration in the standard of other boat owners and even have a few scars to show for it.

From *Punch*, 3 January 1979

· · · — — — · · ·